A CLATTERING BENEATH the WOODS

by

Sally J Hubbard

Blue Poppy Publishing

2020

A Clattering Beneath the Woods

This is a work of fiction. Events and locations are fictional. Characters are not based on any person living or dead.

Cover art and illustrations by Ian Pethers

glenrockstudio.co.uk

Published by Blue Poppy Publishing, Devon

FIRST EDITION 2020

REPRINTED 2021

ISBN – 978-1-911438-68-7

Dedicated to:
Jimmy and Charlie who grew up in the wood;
Keith who tends the wood,
and my Dad, Tony, who believed in all things wonderful...

Chapter One

The wood was softened with blurriness that morning: maybe it was the silvery white threads of spiders' webs, strung across the path from tree to tree which brushed across and caught on Polly's face, wet and sticky; maybe it was the mist clouding over the warmth of the stream in the chilly spring air or maybe it was Polly's tears.

Polly loved her wood and she knew she could lose it.

Everything was changing and Polly did not like it: she felt a sense of panic. The first year in secondary school did not feel exciting or welcoming to her and now her family were in danger of losing their home and their precious woodland: her wood, where she loved to be. The wood was the best part of home to Polly, with its flowers, streams and hidden, mossy places and in her mind she could already see the daffodils and violet petals, brambles and cow parsley being torn apart under the tracks of a mining bulldozer or obliterated by the digging of exploratory shafts. Her parents were arguing about the future, again, and she did not want to listen to it anymore and ran to where she could be alone in her wood.

Polly was enjoying some things about school: netball club was fun and she felt accepted there. Making friends was challenging because apart from the netball team, most of the girls in Polly's year seemed older: they wore mascara, carried shiny handbags with painted nails and bent their exercise books in half or smaller to cram them into their bags. Polly took a ruc sac to school, enjoyed doing sport, even in the rain...and she felt she knew so much more about what was going on in the world around them, than her peers. She knew about the plants, the animals and changing seasons; she did not know about the latest fashion, the coolest music or how to wear shoes which hurt your toes and made you walk like a penguin. She saw the natural world around her...and that made school tough.

Polly did not know why she loved the wood so much. Maybe it was because it was an opposite of the noisy, hot and oppressive corridors in her new secondary school. Not that the wood was quiet: the water in the stream was constantly noisy, sometimes sounding like rain fall, sometimes like music. if you stopped to listen and notice. The birds, especially on a spring morning, could be as loud as a playground...if you listened. Polly did stop to notice and listen and sometimes, as she laid her head on some cushiony moss, not for too long, as the moss in the wood was never dry; she could hear sounds from deep in the soil. She liked to imagine they were made by moles blindly carving out tunnels or badgers moving stones and rocks to make a new home, thudding and clattering.

That morning the light was bright, piercing the tree tops in shafts which lit up the new daffodil buds; they were like green pencils, sharp and straight. It was impossible not to tread them down, so Polly leapt onto the bent bough of the apple tree and kept her feet high in the air. To her right, it appeared that a badger had been at work as the earth was freshly turned and holes looked half dug and abandoned along the bank, by the stream, like the many abandoned remnants of the copper mining industry which had filled this valley, long ago. She noticed such things...she chose to look and notice. The light was dancing; it seemed to reflect in prisms from every surface, from the water of the stream, from the dewy, freshly opened leaves on the primroses and even from the cobwebs. In fact the colours shining from the cobwebs were the brightest of all. Polly saw all this and it helped. She could breathe.

She sat and as the sun warmed the ground, she became aware of the smells on the air. She could smell the soil and the wild garlic: sweet and thick at the same time. Later in the spring the garlic would flower and the white flowers fill the air with their musky scent, however it was way too early for the flowers to be open. In fact, Polly could not see any wild garlic plants at all, she looked around for the source of the smell, but saw nothing, no green and white garlic plants but still the smell, like Mum's lasagne mixed with something earthier, came strongly to her from the trees just below the hillside army of green pencils. What was it?

She walked towards the largest of the trees, where fresh earth had been turned over at the base of a tree trunk which was so huge it must have been hundreds of years old. She sniffed the air. Garlic and mushrooms? Cooking? She rested one arm against the tree and allowed it to take her weight as she sniffed, her face turned to the weak springtime sun.

All of a sudden something knocked into her legs from behind and she fell forward onto her knees. She peered through the bright morning sun back towards the tree. The sunlight was both golden and violet blue...it was hard to see what had knocked her over. She rubbed the twigs and moss from her knees and sat back on her heels. There was an opening in the tree and what looked like a door began to move more slowly, opening further to reveal darkness. As she stared through the bouncing light a person appeared from within the door. A boy, slightly smaller than Polly, moved youthfully and jumped over a muddy mound, threw the basket he held in the air and caught it again, with a laugh. Polly continued to stare at the person, slightly lowering herself to the ground to become below his line of vision. He appeared to be a teenage boy with a mass of black curls which bounced as he jumped. His clothes were old fashioned to Polly: a blue shirt, black trousers which only reached his knees, held up by braces at which he constantly worried, as they slipped from his shoulders.

He turned his back on Polly and began to walk along the muddy path by the stream. The door swung closed behind him and again he threw his basket in the air. It somersaulted, out of control, over his head and towards where Polly was kneeling. She jumped quickly to avoid being hit and the noise alerted the boy. He swung around. They stared at each other. With a sudden movement the boy leapt behind a tree, silhouetted black against the morning sun. The light exploded in gold around the tree; Polly peered into it, screwing her eyes up tight. The early morning light was directly behind the old oak and she could not see either the tree trunk or boy clearly in the dancing, shimmering and glaring gold.

"Can you still see me?" he asked.

"What? Yes...who?" Polly stammered, standing up straight and plotting which way she could run to get away. "No, but you are just behind the tree..."

"Bother. Bother," said the boy, "who are you? From the boat, are you?"

"What?" said Polly, beginning to back away, "who are you? This is my wood. I live here. What do you want? Can I help you?" she asked, aiming her question into the bright sun and trying to be polite, even though she was unnerved.

"I live here. I live here. Can you still see me?"

"Yes. No. What are you doing? Why are you hiding?"

Polly heard the door open again behind her and a shocked older, female voice whisper, "Efrem, Efrem. Come here, come back."

Polly did not know where to look. She was scared to take her eyes from the direction of the boy and also anxious to see who was behind her.

"Marfa," called the boy. "I am sorry. I came out too late. Maybe she is from the boat?"

"Efrem," the voice sounded cross and anxious, "Efrem, walk in the bright light and come back."

"I can help you if you are lost," called Polly who sensed that the two people were more scared of her than she of them, "I am Polly, I live here."

Efrem stepped from behind the tree, "we live here, Polly. I am sorry I knocked you over with the door, it is too heavy. Can I help you?"

"Efrem!" called the voice from inside the tree.

"What do you mean you live here?" asked Polly, moving towards the boy.

I mean this is my home, h...o...m...e," he spoke to her as if she did not understand his language. "I am just gathering roots, allium for the soup, but I was late getting up this morning. Are you from the boat?"

"The boat? What do you mean this is home? Where?" Polly looked around her and back at the doorway. She could not see the owner of the anxious voice.

"I am looking for roots," he spoke even slower, as if talking to a young child, but his eyes were warm and he smiled. Picking up a twig he scratched the soil on the bank of the stream exposing a glossy white root, which he picked and dropped into his basket. To appear friendly, Polly also bent down and dug at the loose soil with her fingers, finding another white root, she offered it to Efrem.

"That's a stinger. A nettle. We want allium," and he took her offering and gently threw it into the frothy, white stream. "Thank you though," he seemed to almost bow slightly and smiled with shining eyes.

"Come and meet my family. If you have news for us, they will be pleased."

"Where? Your family? Where?"

"Here," he pointed towards the door, "my name is Efrem, Salve," and he extended his hand.

"Polly," she answered, "I would love, I think, to meet your family."

"Well, I just need a few more roots, and I will take you inside. Marfa, be easy, Polly could have news," he called towards the tree.

Polly heard a slight exasperated sigh from within and called out, "I will help collect the roots for you!"

She stumbled behind Efrem as he worked on the mossy bank, exposing roots and sometimes tiny bulbs. Polly offered more curly and sleek white roots, but most were rejected. "Allium. Garlic is what we want, but thank you."

With a few handfuls of roots, tangled like spaghetti in the bottom of the reedy basket, some early primrose flowers and some bulbs Polly could not identify, Efrem decided they had enough and turned to her.

"Would you like to see my home?" again he spoke slowly and used his hands to show the way to the door.

"Yes, thank you," Polly replied. She found it hard to be nervous with the boy as his smile was so warm and welcoming.

It took some effort to pull open the heavy door, even though it was small, there was no handle and Efrem had to push his hand into what looked like a normal knot hole in the bark and twist something on the inside. Polly stooped slightly to follow him into a dark corridor which seemed to be built into and beyond the tree trunk. She stepped down some stone steps which were eroded in the centre, presumably from the passage of many feet. The corridor led slightly down hill, so Polly found herself putting her hands out for balance. The sides were dark, mainly constructed of earth, wet to the touch but, occasionally, timber supported the walls and Polly scraped her fingers on the rough wood. The smell of earthy, warm garlic came clearer to them both and after walking for about five minutes in the dark burrow, the space became lighter and the walls drew back to reveal a larger space, entirely underground, lit by some sort of lanterns which gave off a soft glow and sweet smell. The light from the lanterns seemed to change in colour, sometimes there was an orange glow, like that from a bonfire and then it became blue; a soft blue which Polly could not liken to anything she had ever seen before. There were mats on the floor, wooden shelves around the walls supporting a collection of pots, pans and many jars. The jars were topped with large corks and tied down with twine or string which looked like fronds of ivy twisted together. Small jars seemed to contain seeds and larger jars held liquid of many colours, in fact the colours seemed to glow and shimmer in the lantern light. Two rabbits were suspended from the roof, dead and elongated, their eyes misty; three large birds were looped together on a hook near the door. Polly stepped aside to avoid hitting them with her head and tried to hide a grimace of distaste. They were colourful birds and Polly's eye was drawn to the long, rusty coloured tail feathers and blue, green feathers around their necks. Pheasants. It was warm in the room and full of colour; it smelt delicious but most surprising of all was the six people, if people they were, who were gathered around a large range, like the ancient cooker her Gran had in her house. As one, they turned to face Polly and Efrem. Polly felt slightly stunned and could feel her heart beating, but she also saw a warmth in their eyes.

"This is Polly," said Efrem, "I think she must be from the boat. Alba, I am so hungry, them roots must be enough now?" He handed the basket to a girl, possibly a little older than him, who had the same black curls and blue, blue eyes. She was slightly smaller in height than Polly, but broader and her face was that of a girl in her late teens. She was chopping some sort of vegetables on a large blue plate. "Polly," said Efrem, as he sat on a wooden chair by the table and pulled out a chair for her, "this is my mother," he gestured towards a lady, of similar height to her daughter, dressed in a long skirt and shirt, the colour of bluebells; she had an apron around her waist and was scowling at her son and trying to smile at Polly at the same time: her face was a mixture of fighting emotions and she nervously pushed her black curls under a scarf which was wound loosely around her hair.

"The boat," she smiled at Polly, "oh you are welcome, Salve, do sit and eat. It's all but ready." She pointed to a chair and smiled, "If you are from the boat with news," she flashed a scowl at Efrem, "then you are welcome."

An older man sat beside the range in a wooden chair which looked old, warped with age and discoloured by smoke, rather like the man himself. His face had a glum expression which lit up at mention of the boat and he gestured towards the table for Polly to sit. Two younger children, both girls, were playing a game which looked like some adaptation of draughts. They were sat on the mud floor in an orange pool of light cast by the lantern suspended over them. Efrem pointed towards them, "Carita and Mabel," he said, "my sisters," and he made a face at them, sticking out his tongue and squinting down his nose.

"Efrem," his mother reproached, "you are the most fortunate of boys, now don't you forget it."

"The boat? " asked Efrem's father, leaning forward with a look of anticipation. Polly had no idea what they were talking about. She did not know of any boat and was about to tell them when a loud clanging and banging sounded from the roof, from the walls, all around them. Polly jumped up in fear, but the others did not respond with any show of surprise or nerves, just a look of weariness and with some irritation. Efrem's father turned away from Polly, his look of anticipation replaced with sadness and walked towards a further door, set deep at the back, black of the room. "Such a clattering, 'tis blocked again, clattering, clattering," he grumbled, "I'm coming!" he called, in the general direction of the door and left with a deep sigh. No-one moved and all seemed to be listening with their eyes focussed on the door. Polly felt nervous. After a few minutes the loud, metallic clanging stopped and the door opened. The old man resumed his seat and once again the only sounds were the bubbling pot on the range, the chattering of the two smaller girls and the hiss of lanterns on the walls.

"There, there Pa," said Mabel, the smallest girl who lifted her arms to be picked up by her father, "'Tis because we have the very sweetest, that's why it is stuck."

"I wish that were true, Mabel, my petal, I wish," her father replied, tousling her black curls. He tried to smile at his daughter, but his forehead remained creased with lines of worry. He wiped at the oil and sweat on his face and rubbed his hands down his coarse breeches.

The family sat to eat around a large table and a dish was laid for Polly. It was all so extraordinary, so fascinating, that she allowed herself to be waited upon, to be served a creamy coloured soup: she smiled and thanked them and was only faintly aware that they had misidentified her and that she needed to tell them she was not from the "boat" but actually lived in the nearby house with her family, who had no idea at all about the existence of these strange, wood people.

"It's lovely," she said politely to the older girl, Alba, who had served her; the creamy soup was full of the tastes of garlic, mushroom and possibly cream. It was savoury, smooth and one of the most delicious foods Polly had tasted. It seemed to smell and taste of the wood.

"Wait," Alba said kindly, "we add our own theri, here," and she passed a jug to Polly which contained a thick, dark, shiny liquid. She was not sure what to do with it, but aware the family were watching and waiting for the jug.

"I have not put in any theri, we add our own, as much as you want, Polly," Alba encouraged, speaking slowly, like Efrem, as if they were explaining something very basic to someone who did not understand.

"Aye," the father added, encouragingly, "certainly as much as you want."

Polly became aware that she should pour some of the oily liquid into her soup, so she splashed a little into the centre, thanked Alba and handed the jug, blue like all the rest of the pots and pans, to Efrem who poured a huge amount into his soup, until the liquid skimmed the brim and he had to mop at the table with a cloth his mother handed to him, tutting her reproach.

"'Tis not good unless you have lots," he said to Polly and handed the jug back. Polly allowed another glutinous, splosh of the liquid to land in her delicious soup and, following Efrem's lead, stirred the oil into the creamy deliciousness, until it all became brown and very unappetising. She took a mouthful and felt her lips draw back into a grimace. Covering up her rudeness as quickly as she could, she turned her head, coughed and mumbled, "excuse me, I have a bit of a cold." In fact her savoury soup had become, because of the theri, so sweet and cloying that she was having trouble swallowing it and fought back a desire to retch. She blushed with embarrassment and was quite amazed to see the whole family, in turn, pour so much of the sweet oil into their delicious soups, turning the creamy loveliness into sludge. Polly knew she could not eat it and felt a slight panic about being with these people, under a tree, under her wood. For the first time she felt totally out of place.

"I am so sorry," she said. "I have remembered I need to go. I am meeting someone."

Her face reddened and she stood up and wiped her mouth on her sleeve. The soup stuck onto her jumper like toffee or jam and bits of fluff were stuck to her lip. "I must go now, but thank you so much," she smiled at Alba and then the parents who were looking at her with disappointment and some surprise.

"The boat?" asked Efrem's father, "we need to know."

"Umm, yes," mumbled Polly, again blushing and feeling sweat break out on her forehead. "I..." she rubbed at the bits of fluff stuck to her lips and teeth.

At that moment, as if on cue to save her embarrassment, the clanging and jarring sounds began again. The walls seemed to shake as if a battering ram was thudding, over and over, trying to break them into pieces. The jars knocked together on the shelves and the dead birds and rabbits swayed above their heads. The whole family groaned, but only Efrem's father stopped eating the sludgy, gloop and stood wearily. "Clatter, clatter, I'm a coming. Efrem, you need to help me this time. I could not have cleared it right last time. The soup will stay warm." He turned to Polly. "'Tis a worrying, worrying time. You will be back? Tomorrow?"

"Oh, of course," said Polly, relieved at her opportunity to escape without having to eat and even more relieved to get away from the noise which sounded like the burrow would soon cave in. "Of course," she added decisively, as if it had always been her plan, as if she had a plan and as if she knew all about the family, their boat and the problems with the clattering and clanging. "Of course," she called to the retreating figure of the father and Efrem as they headed towards the door, deep in the back of the room. She nodded her head again, wiped her mouth on the back of her hand, smiled her thanks at the family and made her way to the corridor. Once in the darkness of the burrow, she put her hands over her head to shield herself from the avalanche of noise above her and ran, ran... to the heavy door and through it to the wood: her wood.

As she pushed the door shut behind her, not an easy thing to do, she stopped and stared at the tree. She could no longer hear the thudding and clattering, but how had she never seen the door before? The door did sit far back in the trunk and thick, ropes of ivy hung down over it, but it did seem beyond belief that she had never noticed it before. It was right there! So easy to see! As she stared she became aware of a plaque, partially covered with moss and lichen which was nailed onto the tree a few inches above the door. Bark had grown around it, so it seemed part of the tree. She scraped at the green mould until it revealed a sign, made of metal, on which she could eventually, after more scraping with a sharp twig, make out some sort of inscription.

Latchley Theriaca Dulcis Fodina CDX

As Polly lay in bed that night she felt very alive; she would return the next day and explain to the family of wood people that she knew nothing about a boat. She did not want to deceive them; they were nice people. But who were they? She strained her ears to listen for the clattering and banging, but could hear nothing but the safe sounds of her home: a radio muffled downstairs, a window creaking and the dishwasher sploshing below her in the kitchen.

Theriaca? Dulcis? Fod? What had it said on the plaque?

Chapter Two

"We'll have to sell, Lara, I can't see how we can make any more from the land without a huge capital investment. Money we don't have." Polly's father and mother were talking, in a very low dejected way, as they ate porridge and drank coffee at breakfast. It was a discussion she knew well and had heard many times before. She stopped on the stairs to listen. The family of three were struggling with money and their hopes of making a living from the fields and wood which belonged to them were being squashed. They had hoped to make money from the daffodils which bloomed each year in the wood; they were the naturalised remnants of a vast industry which had covered the Tamar Valley a hundred years ago, when there had been open fields where now stood her precious wood. A mixture of native trees, broad leafed and fruit trees now made the soil below damp and mossy. They prevented the sun from fully reaching the ground. Only in one area, where ancient cherry trees clung to life, also a part of a former industry, was there sufficient light to penetrate the dusk to transform the hillside into a glory of wild, pale daffodils each spring. The cherry trees were over a hundred years old apparently, according to the old lady in the village who had once been employed to pick fruit on the land, many years ago, when she could walk without her cane. The valley had been a major producer of apples, cherries, daffodils and soft fruit, but modern, mass production of flowers in heated poly tunnels and uniform shaped fruit had replaced the ancient varieties. Polly liked the names of the old apple trees: Ben's Red and Cornish Pippin and Pig's Snout. The apple and cherry trees were now bent over at strange angles, bore little fruit and the area of daffodils grew smaller each year, even though Polly's father cut trees carefully to allow in the light and added fertiliser to the soil. They had hoped to sell the pale, lily like flowers and their bulbs, but each year there were fewer to sell and less money to be made.

They had tried to rear pigs for profit, chickens, turkeys at Christmas time and even llamas whose silky fleeces could, apparently, be turned into beautiful clothes. All ideas had failed, however, for the simple reason that there was not enough land to make anything truly profitable. Three pigs, two llamas, a handful of chickens, two sacks of daffodil bulbs did not pay the bills or mortgage.

"I know we don't want to leave or lose the wood," said Polly's father, "but you come up with an alternative! I can't think of anything."

As usual, such discussions led to irritation and grumbling and it was this which upset Polly the most. Her father had been made redundant from his job in a nearby College. They had hoped that the land could have generated enough to compensate for his loss of income, but all ideas had only returned pocket money or even worse, run at a loss. Now they had been approached by a mining consultant, Mr Dominus, who wanted to explore the possibility of reopening long closed copper and tin mines whose flooded tunnels ran under the wood. Such exploration would mean sinking shafts under the cherry trees and tearing up the daffodil bulbs to test the soil beneath. The mossy, flower strewn peace would be replaced by industrial vehicles, noise, mud and people. The mewing buzzards, badgers and secretive, sensitive deer would leave and be replaced by people. Mr Dominus was offering a great deal of money, however, and should his explorations prove successful, the family could at least stay in their home, but they would have to sell the wood to the mining company. It was a big decision to make and it saddened the family to even contemplate it.

"What if we build a larger chicken house and sell eggs daily to the supermarkets? "Her mother asked, "I have a friend who did just that."

"How do we build the house, buy the chickens? Where does that money come from? We are just dreaming. We need to move into a smaller house with no land, or sell the wood to Mr Dominus. Then we can stay. "

"No land?" Lara's face was grey and sad, "and if we sell the wood, won't we have mining trucks, people and noise right outside the window?" She pointed to the kitchen window where a robin was eating nuts from a feeder and there was nothing to be seen beyond, but green fields.

"Land costs money and it is not paying its way. The land, the wood is not making any money for us. We need to move, or sell the wood," he grumbled, "we have been through all this before. Mr Dominus is coming to have a discussion next week. Let's see what he says."

"Oh!"

It all sounded a little too definite, so Polly jumped, noisily, down the last three steps and ran into the kitchen in an attempt to end a conversation she did not want to hear and maybe, therefore, make it all go away.

"Morning Poll," smiled Lara, her mother, "come and eat up quickly. You are late this morning."

Her father walked past her, tousled her hair and stopped to pull at a twig of ivy, firmly knotted in Polly's blonde hair.

"Ivy, Poll? What have you been up to?" Before she could answer he walked out to the porch where all the wellingtons and wet weather clothes were stored, pulled on a jacket and boots and, with a sigh, went outside.

"Oh Dad, I'll feed the chickens," she called, ignoring the bowl of porridge held out to her and the surprised expressions of her parents. "I'll feed them, you have... have, another coffee!" she smiled, trying to make it sound as if she offered to do the chores every day.

"Go ahead," said her father, pulling off a muddy wellington boot and padding back to the kitchen table in his socks, "I'm always up for another cup of coffee. What have you done wrong, Poll? All a bit suspicious I think," he laughed, but he was not going to pursue Polly's reasons for suddenly offering to help, so she ran outside and after putting a scoop of feed in the chickens' run and opening the door of their house to let them out, she ran up into the wood and along the path towards the tree.

The grass was very damp, the moss underfoot was springy and full of moisture, the leaves obliterating the morning sun. She wondered if the door would still be there. The cold morning air and spots of rain all made it feel highly unlikely. As she reached the tree and the daffodil spikes, at the end of the path, the sun broke through the clouds and shone down through the trees in clearly defined rays, just as a child would draw the sunshine: a golden river fragmented by the dark trees. The tree was soothed in the warm sunshine and there, Polly could see, facing the morning sun, was the door and above it the plaque. It was real!

She pulled a piece of paper and a pen from her pocket and wrote down the inscription: Latchley Theriaca Dulcis Fodina CDX

What did it mean? Latchley was the name of the village, but the other words held no meaning for her. She carefully folded the paper and put it in her pocket and leaned in close to the door to listen, pressing her ear to the prickly bark. She would have loved to have knocked and entered the strange dwelling, but knew that her parents would be suspicious of the time she had taken to feed the chickens. She heard nothing, all was quiet. Could she smell the lovely garlic soup which they had so ruined? No, the air was sweetened by the gentle scent of the wood: damp soil and moss, maybe foxes, but no smell of cooking or soup. Polly ran home, ate porridge at speed and ran for the school bus, the strange words safe in her pocket.

LATCHLE
THERIACA
CDX

Chapter Three

School dragged. The early sun, so hopeful in the morning wood, had been replaced by a thick, soaking drizzle and school was always worse when it was raining. The corridors were packed full of children at break and lunch as it was too cold and wet to go outside. The air was warm, wet and suffocating. Children milled about, bored and cold. There were some groups who sat in corners of rooms playing games, chatting, but these were mainly girls who all seemed to know each other, who wore lipstick and mascara and had all their books stuffed into a tiny, shiny hand bag... and Polly could not join them. They were alien beings.

Boys tended to wander in groups, looking for something to do, like packs of puppies trying to be wolves. Polly was walking the corridors with Will, a boy she knew from her primary school. Will was feeling particularly nervous and insignificant, having had a chip thrown at him by a boy in the canteen: a boy who looked, to Will, more like a man. He looked far too old for school.

"Catch!" the older boy with stubble on his chin, had yelled and when the chip bounced off Will's hair, landing on the floor, the older students had roared with appreciation. When Will was made to pick it up by an angry looking dinner lady who had managed to entirely miss the actual event, the older boys sneered and laughed again.

"Don't leave your mess on the floor; we always put our rubbish in the bin here. You will need to learn that very soon!" she scowled, her face tired and hot. She did not meet his eyes. She did not try to understand.

"It's not..." Will began to explain but realised that she was not going to listen or care about the true account of the chip. So he picked it up and placed it in an overflowing bin in front of jeering boys, who tossed their hair, spoke too loudly and sought the attention of anyone who would deign to look their way.

Walking down the history corridor Polly was jostled by older students, who seemed to find it hilarious, and she fell into the history room, the door flying back and hitting a shelf with a loud crash. "Hey!" shouted the teacher who was sitting at his desk eating a sausage roll while marking a pile of exercise books. "If you can't behave you can come and spend lunchtime in here with me, in silence!"

The teacher sounded stressed and distracted. The door had obviously been flung open a few times before.

"Actually I'd love to be in here out of this chaos," she said quietly, more to her friend Will, than to the teacher.

"What?" the teacher, Mr Smith replied, half raising his head from the pile of exercise books, decorated with various Tudor Kings and Queens. He was trying to smile, but looked tired and stressed.

"Nothing, sorry Sir," muttered Polly going out into the frantic corridor and leaving behind the peace of the room.

"Where shall we go?" asked Will, dodging an older boy who was chasing another, apparently in possession of a football which did not belong to him.

"Library?" said Polly. She was not a keen reader, but the library was heavily supervised at lunchtimes, by a fierce librarian, a library assistant and sixth formers. Consequently, the older, football chasing, laughing and pushing boys were never to be seen near the place. It was a sanctuary on such a day.

"Library," agreed Will, who was small for his age, not yet entirely happy in the new, big school and who clung to his old friend in a way which was comforting to Polly at times, but also could be very irritating.

The library was quite full, it being a rainy day. They dodged two older boys on the stairs who casually put out their legs to trip any Year 7s who had not learnt how to negotiate the minefield corridors. They smiled at the scowling teacher on duty outside, who told them initially, "library is full," then having noticed the rather lost and desperate look on their faces, had opened the door and virtually pushed them in. " Oh, go on. Room for two little ones." She patted them on their heads, causing both to jerk their heads away and blush scarlet. The teacher's kindness simply made them feel even more out of place.

Feeling as small and frazzled as they could possibly feel, the two found a corner of the library, behind a carousel of spinning books and sat down, sharing a comfy armchair. At first they did not speak, but simply breathed: it was safe here. No older students with loud voices or cringing teachers with sugary smiles to upset them. Around them was a display, hanging from the ceiling, showing pictures and maps of an archaeological dig which was taking place nearby. "Students Help Archaeologists Find Roman Wall" was the title, written on a large suspended piece of cardboard which was meant to be tethered at both ends to the ceiling, but which had been broken free at one end and now hung down, making everyone have to duck underneath. The sign was decorated with pictures of roman remains and cuttings from the local newspaper. Students' work was on other display boards and varied from pictures of Romans walking around the Tamar Valley, complete with their armour, swords and eagle headed standards, to newspaper articles about roman life, a picture of the Coliseum, roman emperors and gladiators. Older students had been studying the impact of the Romans on the Celtic community of the Tamar Valley, but neither Polly nor Will were aware of any local amphitheatres with lions and fighting slaves, as suggested in the display.

The caption underneath read: "The Tamar Valley, Cornwall. In Roman Times."

"That ain't right," Will said, pointing to the picture and nudging Polly in the ribs.

"Coliseum's in Rome...I think," she agreed, "or Athens?"

"Ain't flaming well here," replied Will. "This is Cornwall, not Italy!"

"Silly idiots," said Polly and both giggled, pleased that they could criticise the work of their elders, even though it was behind their backs. It made the shoves, pushes, lipstick and flying chips slightly easier to bear.

Polly looked quietly at the display work to find something else to ridicule when she saw, suspended from the display with a drawing pin, a piece of writing, supposedly a diary, written by a Year 9 student, Amy Collins. She read:

"CDX Aprilis. Dies Lunae.

Anglia is too cold for me and my family. Its horrid and we plan to return to somewhere warm."

Polly stopped reading and looked again at the title. CDX. CDX. Where had she seen this? She remembered, it had been written on the plaque.

"What does CDX mean?" she asked Will who had picked up a book to read, a well read and slightly tatty copy of the Guinness Book of Records. Will glanced up, "not sure," he mumbled, "probably Latin, you know Roman."

"Latin?" asked Polly. "Latin for what?"

"It's a number I think," replied Will, looking at a picture of a man with seven-foot-long finger nails, "they are called roman numerals."

Polly's face became animated and excited, "come on, come with me to see that History teacher. He might be able to help."

"With what?" asked Will, who did not want to leave his safe corner until the bell sounded for lessons and the corridors began to clear, "I have had enough chips today. Look at this... he is the world's smallest man."

Polly shared her friend's anxiety about the corridors on a wet lunchtime and instead decided to speak to the scary librarian. She now felt sure the plaque had Roman numerals and that the language was Latin. The beak nosed librarian was telling some other children to leave the library, having been too noisy, when Polly interrupted: "Do we have books about Latin or Romans please?"

"Pardon?" she said, not looking up, her glasses slipping down her aquiline nose.

"Latin books, do we have any?" Eventually she heard Polly and seemed pleased to have an enquiry about Latin. Looking at her over her reading glasses with new admiration, she pointed towards the back of the library, "there are books about Roman life, Latin translation books and classical civilisation. What are you studying in History?"

"Oh, it's just for my own interest," she smiled, feeling a little like a creep, "we are not studying the Romans."

"Oh my," she replied, "well Latin for Beginners is right there, dear."

Blushing at the use of the word "dear" she nodded her thanks and found the book. Maybe the words were in Latin? Pulling out the piece of paper in her pocket she looked again at the inscription from the plaque.

Latchley Theriaca Dulcis Fodina CDX

She searched the words in alphabetical order and was delighted to find the word "Dulcis." So it was

Latin! She read:

Dulcis: sweet.

Eagerly she looked for the next word: Fodina. The closest translation she could find was:

Fodere: To mine.

Then she looked for Theriaca and found a direct translation:

Theriaca: Treacle

To mine sweet treacle. Is that what it meant?

The back of the book had all the roman numerals listed with their modern counterparts.

CDX : 410

So the inscription was Latin and it was something about mining sweet treacle in 410?

"Dear!" shouted the Librarian. Polly ignored her. "Hey!" shouted the librarian, all attempts at being polite and caring forgotten, "the bell has gone, and you are late and will get a detention... and I need the library cleared. Now!" She was obviously not a lady to be ignored.

"To mine sweet treacle in Latchley...Latchley sweet treacle mine," mumbled Polly as she walked past the irritated librarian, her mind not registering any of her threats. "Bye," she beamed at her and was sure she heard a growl back.

Chapter Four

As soon as possible, after arriving home on the school bus, Polly told her mother that she was going to walk to the river. The River Tamar is wide near Latchley with many dark path ways under the tall coniferous trees. The main tracks are frequented often by foresters, dog walkers and possibly salmon poachers, but many relics of the mining past of the valley can be glimpsed through the undergrowth: granite walls, fenced off mine shafts and metal tram lines. Polly's mother was thumbing, despondently, through estate agent leaflets and merely looked up and smiled. Some leaflets had slipped down from the table and lay discarded on the floor, unwanted.

"Dinner won't be until about 7, when Dad gets back from," she nearly said work, but stopped herself in time to say, "when Dad gets back." Polly knew her father had been to see a local primary school head teacher, with a view to being offered some supply work. All this concerned her, but the need to go into the wood, find Efrem and talk to him, stopped her feeling unduly worried for the family's circumstances.

"See you in a bit," she mumbled and, instead of walking towards the Tamar, she set off for the wood. It was unusual for her to visit the wood at dusk, but she wanted to see the plaque and possibly the family; she was not sure what she had to say to them.

The door way was still there, with the plaque more evident after her rough scraping the previous night. She thought to knock and wait and then decided that might seem rude and wondered what she could offer as a gift. Garlic roots? It was all she could think of, so she began scrambling in the soil on the bank of the stream where the garlic plants were beginning to show.

"You having allium for your tea too?" came a voice behind her. It was Alba, as dark as Polly was fair; she was stood up to her knees in the stream, her feet bare and her blue skirt held up with thick string. She was holding a basket, the same one Efrem had filled with roots the night before, and in the straw basket were long, fish like creatures, slithering and sliding about. Polly started: "Oh, what are they?" she asked pointing and taking a step back.

"What?"

"Those fish?" Polly said, regaining some composure.

"Eels," she said pointing to the long, slithery, snake like creatures, "and I got one brown trout," Alba held up a small fish with a look of triumph.

"You catch the eels?" asked Polly. She had caught little fish near the waterfall, but never these long, slithery, slightly repulsive creatures. Alba looked at her with some surprise and, as Efrem had done, spoke slowly in her explanation, as if Polly was an alien being... which indeed she was.

"In Spring time we have lots of eels here. They make a good stew, but I like the brown trout best. Eels have such big bones. 'Tis hard to eat 'em," Alba held up a wriggling, gyrating eel as she spoke, it flapped its wet body on her arm and Polly drew away even more.

"Comin' down to see Pater? He is so worried about the clattering and really hoped you would be back. I did say we had not seen you before and it was unlikely."

Polly felt concern again that she had been misidentified and although reluctant to go near the eels, she nodded to Alba and followed her, at a safe distance, towards the door in the tree.

"I have garlic for you," she offered tentatively, holding out some white roots, "Allium?"

"Gratias Tibi, thank you, allium, garlic, it's the same and we do use it a great deal." Polly could see that Alba was being gracious, as her gift was poor, but she liked the girl more for her kindness in accepting such a soiled and sparse offering. Picking up a long thin straw basket, with a narrow neck opening to a wide bottle like structure, which appeared to have been used to catch the eels, the girls pushed open the heavy door in the tree trunk.

In the kitchen the mother was cutting vegetables while the father seemed to be mending a large metal object which was lying on hessian sacks. The smaller girls could be heard, laughing, in an adjoining room. Efrem was nowhere to be seen.

"Salve, welcome, Polly," said the mother, holding out her hand, "maybe we can introduce ourselves properly today. I am Mistress Tremellin and there is Master Tremellin. You are from the Mill and we dearly hope you have news of the boat?"

Master Tremellin nodded his greeting and held his greasy hands up to show he could not shake hands.

"We are in dire need to know when the boat is coming," he said with a look of great respect, "Efrem has gone to ask the other families near here if they have news. He will be home soon. I doubt they will know. It seems an age and so very, very unusual." He spoke very slowly and with a look of deep concern which spread to the Mistress and she began to wring her hands on her floury apron and push her curls under her scarf.

Polly did not want to deceive them any longer, but with no knowledge of boats, clattering or their problems, she felt she had to introduce herself properly before their expectations rose further.

"It is very good to meet you both," she turned to Alba who was doing something indescribable to the eels in the sink, "and you too, Alba, it's a real pleasure."

She knew she sounded too formal, but was trying hard to find the words to explain who she was. It was difficult, when she did not really understand who they were....

"I am sorry, I am not..." she began, only to be interrupted by a loud thump which seemed to come from the back wall of the kitchen. It was as if someone was hitting the wall with a huge piece of wood. Polly jumped and grabbed hold of the back of a chair. The thumping grew louder and was joined with the clanging of metal, a jarring, harsh sound as metal screeched on metal. Polly could not tell where the sound came from; it was now all around her...it was frightening and Polly looked towards the door, her possible escape route. The banging and clanging seemed to increase in speed and rhythm and Polly moved towards the entrance as the back door flung open and Efrem appeared, looking strained and red in the face, "Come on Pa, it's the Big Un!"

"Polly, come with us. I'll keep you safe. You can see the problem for yourself," said Master Tremellin. He grabbed a pair of thick gloves from a high shelf and opening the door wide, allowed a rather nervous and stunned Polly to pass ahead of him into a dark corridor, which resonated with thunder.

The corridor more resembled a mine tunnel than a part of a house and after walking by the light of lanterns, glowing a pale orange in the walls, they came upon a steep ladder, made of wood which dropped down a sheer shaft. It was with a great deal of fear in her voice that Polly asked if they were to descend the ladder.

"Efrem will go first and I'll go behind.... a good ladder, strong and safe...just hold tight," shouted the Master. He needed to shout as the metallic clanging and thumping was now even louder and joined by a sound like water falling over a waterfall, but not in the friendly way the stream fell softly over the fall near Polly's house. The thumping sound now seemed to Polly to match her thumping heart beats as she descended the wooden ladder, fastening each of her hands like a vice on each rung. After a time, she found impossible to quantify, such was her fear, the group emerged into a large cavern lit again by pale lanterns. Along one stone wall were huge wheels, like cartwheels, fastened with shining copper. As Polly grew more used to the dim light she saw there were many doors around the cavern, of various heights and states of repair. Each was open, or being flung open, and from each more men and boys appeared. They were all dressed like Efrem and his father, in working clothes, overalls, jackets and breeches. All had dark curly, black hair, were of similar height, no taller than Polly herself, and shared the same look of concern. Some youths ran quickly to the nearest wheel and began to turn them, two to a wheel, pulling the rungs around in a clockwise direction; older men and some who looked very old indeed, walked more slowly to a wheel and turned to Efrem for advice.

"It's the Big Un!" he yelled above the thumping and shouting. "We need to divert it to all the pipes which run over the Tiddy Brook." There were some nods of agreement.

The gathered group, with the exception of Polly, understood immediately what Efrem had said and moved away from some wheels to turn others. It took six men and a crow bar to move one particularly jammed wheel and the men were sweating and groaning as they forced the cogs to turn. As they worked, Polly drew back and watched. The men worked quietly now and with an order. They all knew what to do and as they worked the clattering receded, slowly at first and then with a huge whoosh, loud enough to make Polly cry out, the noise stopped. The men secured the wheels in their new positions, wiped their brows and gathered in groups.

"So have you heard anything? "

"Someone needs to go see Cap'n...."

"Yes, soon, needs to be soon..."

"Never happened..."

"The Big Un will blow...I shan't sleep tonight..."

" Time we gave up, lads..."

This last sombre comment killed any conversation and the men turned to go back the way they had come. Efrem came over to Polly with his father, pleased that he had correctly diagnosed the problem. Polly's amazement and shock at all she had seen, loosened her tongue and in a garble she almost shouted at the pair, "I am Polly, I live near the wood, it's my wood actually...I am not from a boat, I don't know about a boat...I can't help you and I don't know who you are or what is happening here and I'm scared and I think I need to go home and..." All the time she spoke, Polly was listening for more thunderous sounds and looking all around her to see if more doors would fly open and more danger approach.

Master Tremellin placed a hand on her shoulder, he was sweating and looked very disappointed by Polly's explanation, "ah, not from the boat? I know the house at the end of the wood. We don't venture down there too much. Never in daylight. Never worry. It's our mistake and we are sorry we jumped to conclusions so quick, but we are worried. It's nothing to do with you. Please forget we asked."

"What are you so worried about and what on earth is that awful sound and the wheels and..." Polly realised she was beginning to gabble again and stopped herself to smile at the Master, who had been gracious in his disappointment.

"I am sorry, Sir," she said. "If I could help you, I would, but I am not sure what the problem is...or even where I am!" As she spoke the cavern emptied of men and, with the clattering gone, it became a wondrous space, of orange glows, strange metal workings and she noticed the sweetness of the air, like the scent of new daffodils.

"The theri boat has not come for such a time..." said Efrem, explaining, as he gasped for breath.

"Theri?" questioned Polly, remembering her Latin discoveries, "you mean, er, treacle?" she asked, expecting to be laughed at.

"Yes, 'tis the theri pipes which are clogged ...I do not know how to explain. The pipes are so full; the theri can't go anywhere, as the boat has not come."

Polly tried to follow the explanation. It did seem to involve treacle, or something which went by the name of treacle. She was stood in an underground cave, with strange men who used strange Latin words, who lived under her wood and were terrified of the booming sound made by huge pipes of copper. She did not understand and looked at them with a questioning expression, her mouth hanging open.

"Let's show her Wheal Kitty, Pater. She doesn't really understand what 'tis all about."

With a kindly nod, Master Tremellin led the two to another door, built of thick, dark wood at the far side of the cave. Again, it concealed a shaft with a wooden ladder. Polly did not need to ask if they were going to descend, but set off behind Efrem, still holding each rung tightly as she went down. The air was warm and thick; it made her sweat and her lips tasted sweet and salty at the same time. The light grew dimmer and at one point, Efrem called a halt and lit a candle which was fastened to a blue china holder in a cleft in the stone wall.

They stepped off the ladder into a smaller cavern and it took a while for Polly to be able to see anything.

"Keep back, to the side, lass," said Master Tremellin, "Efrem will light the lantern, then you can see your feet." He put out an arm to hold Polly back and she willingly stood still until a warm, orange glow lit the little cave. She was stood on a stone ledge; the words KITTY had been scratched on the far wall and she looked around for something remarkable, trying to understand why they had brought her here.

"Look down, Polly, look down," said Efrem and she looked and saw, only a few feet before them, a pool of liquid, a pool of dark, slowing moving and swirling liquid. Bubbles rose to the surface and broke, slowly, like custard in a pan. As each bubble broke the gelatinous surface, a smell of sweetness rose; a smell of thick, sweet sugar, like a Christmas pudding or heavily scented flowers. She was astounded.

"What is it?" she asked quietly, almost whispering.

"Theri," said Efrem, "the best in Cornwall and this here is the best mine of all. Kitty has the sweetest theri and she never dries up. Here taste!" He leaned down; putting a knee by the side of the pool he stretched a finger into the blackness. He licked his finger and smiled, "you try," he encouraged. Polly followed his example, tentatively kneeling by the moving pool and putting her finger into the warm, oily blackness, trying to avoid the bubbles which splashed thick droplets on the surface of the pool. She drew out her finger, coated in a thick, sticky liquid. She looked at it, she sniffed it and then she licked it.

"It's treacle!" she shouted and put another finger into the gloop, to make sure. "It is treacle! Treacle like you put in cakes...it is, isn't it? That dark treacle which you put in fruit cakes? Isn't it?"

"Why of course," said Master Tremellin, a little surprised at her ignorance. "Call it treacle if you wish, we call it theri and have done so for many, many years. But yes, this..."

"You mine treacle...you are treacle miners...this is a treacle mine..." mumbled Polly, thinking aloud.

"Well course we do, what did you think?"asked Efrem.

"There is a treacle mine under my wood, this is a treacle mine, these are treacle miners..." Polly continued, almost talking to herself and smiling at the wonder of it all.

"Yes, but we are in trouble," said Master Tremellin. Polly stopped smiling, "look here, Kitty is never empty, the theri, she bubbles up from deep in the core of the world and never stops. See, look, the level never changes."

"Why doesn't she overflow?" asked Polly, beginning to refer to the mine as "she" like the miners. "Why doesn't the treacle reach the roof?"

"Because we pipe it away. Kitty has the biggest pipe, the one we call Big Un, look hard, over there, in the corner..."

Polly looked and saw the very tip of a gleaming copper pipe. It must have been about three feet wide and treacle was flowing easily into it, like water over rocks, like a river of ink, glistening and black.

"The Big Un is here 'cos Kitty has the most theri, that big pipe takes it away and then delivers it to smaller pipes and then to the barrelling yard."

"We have so many pipes flowing here, Polly," interjected Efrem, enthusiastically. "We have so much theri. 'Tis the best mine here. Pater says, in other mines, on Bodmin moor, they have nothing like so much as Kitty!"

"So, what is the problem?" asked Polly and Efrem's smile faded quickly.

"All the pipes are full, all the barrels are full, and the boat has not come to take the theri down the river to sell," explained Master Tremellin. We have made more barrels and everything we can fill with theri, is full. Bottles and pans and baths are full of theri. The yard is full...it's loaded in bedrooms and corridors...but the pipes are so full they clog up. We have to keep diverting it round other pipes, every time they clang and clash, they are blocked, and we must be quick...or they could burst."

"Is that what you are doing with the wheels up there?" asked Polly pointing to the ceiling.

"Yes," said Efrem, "we try to find out which pipe is full and divert the treacle," he said the word slowly," to other pipes. A pipe did burst last week, and poor old Ether was hurt by the metal flying back...he's still in bed, with a bad back."

"We don't like to waste theri, 'tis good and we need the sovereigns it brings to pay the rent, but sometimes we have had to let some just seep out into the ground, haven't we Pa?" said Efrem, sadly. "The boat, she should come every Monday to the weir below the village. Unless it is too moonlit, too bright a night, she comes. We take a week's worth of barrels to her and the Cap'n gives us the sovereigns we have earnt from the previous week. But she just hasn't come...no word...nothing."

"It's not right, to let good theri just soak into the ground, when you have to open a pipe and let it go, throw it away. We had to let some go last night or I think the Big Un would have blown..." and he clapped his hands to show the explosion which could have happened.

"You take the barrels through the village? Why have I not seen you?" she asked.

"Because we use..." said Efrem.

"Because we are secretive," answered Master Tremellin, turning away to the ladder. "Are you sure you cannot help us? You know nothing of the boat?"

"Secretive?" questioned Polly.

"Aye," he nodded, "Aye, we are secretive."

Polly looked down, the swirling black, sweet goodness did just keep coming and keep going, down the pipe, down Big Un into a system of pipes which she could only think might resemble the London Underground. The complicated confusion of the map of the Underground, which she had seen on a visit to London, swirled into her mind and she imagined it resembled the system of big, small and intertwining treacle pipes, all carrying their loads of treacle deep down, below the wood.

"Have another taste, if you wish," said the Master, "Efrem, bring us a pot for the eels, before we go back home." He picked up a china bowl which was hidden in another cleft in the rock face, out of sight, and knelt and scooped up a bowl of the liquid, still bubbling in the bowl.

"Let's go up," said the Master, "we have eels for tea and theri to sweeten them....lots of theri," he added ironically.

Chapter Five

It was a few days before Polly saw the family of treacle miners again. Life was busy: there were assessments in school, homework clubs, netball clubs and even a family visit to a cottage which was for sale in the next village. No one had liked it.

Mr Dominus had visited with a team of geologists. Polly only saw him from her bedroom window, a tall man, who stood erect and confident. His hair was dark and straight, and he wore a long, black coat. Resembling a huge crow, he had walked towards her wood, with a clipboard and briefcase.

"I don't like him," she had said to her mother, "he looks mean and I don't want him to have our wood."

"Don't say that, Polly, you didn't even speak to him! He was very polite, very pleasant. He does think there could still be copper and tin below the wood. I know it's sad...I am so sorry...but he does seem excited about buying the wood, for a lot of money! We could stay here, in the house, Poll."

"It will be ruined. What about the daffodils...they have been there for over a hundred years! And the cherry tree. And the violets and primroses..."

"I know, I know," Polly's mother sighed deeply, "he says they would make as little mess as possible..."

"He's already made quite a mess, Mum..." moaned Polly, referring to some large holes which had been dug near a badger sett she knew was in use.

Polly had not forgotten the miners and was worried about their boat, but it all seemed beyond her, beyond anything she could do. It was all beginning to feel very unreal, a blurry dream which had nothing to do with school, home, money problems and homework. It was a problem she could not fully grasp and which did not belong to her. However, she remembered the miners' problems with a rush of emotion when her father walked into the kitchen for tea one evening, having been working in the wood, looking at the swathes of daffodil buds.

"Wish we could sell those flowers, Lara, they will be so beautiful...and there are so many!"

"Well, we could sell bunches of them at the end of the track...they are not going to make a fortune though," she replied, "we have tried."

"The wood smells so sweet this evening. The spring flowers, the soil, I don't know...but it smells like perfume."

"Wow, it's not like you to notice..." Lara smiled.

"No, but it is extraordinary this evening, the air, the breeze, it's a cold breeze but is just full of sweetness, like someone has poured sugar all over the ground." Polly ran, she knew what the sweet smell was...the miners were dumping their treacle. She ran.

Knocking loudly at the door, Polly did not wait for an answer, but fumbled her way along the stone and earth corridor to the family's kitchen. They were all there, sitting looking at a map on the worn and stained table.

"You have had to dump theri?" she asked, noting their looks of anxiety. The atmosphere was tense, there was a stillness and a caution in the air.

"Dump? You mean we have had to let theri out of the pipes? Aye," said Efrem, "Big Un and about three, no four other pipes were fit to burst. We kept divertin' and divertin' but we couldn't stop the clattering." Efrem's face and clothes were black and his face was sweaty and flushed.

"There was nowhere for it to go, see," said his mother, "so we had to open a pipe and let some out. 'Tis terrible shame...so wasteful...all them sovereigns..." her hand went to her mouth and her eyes were all worry and sadness. "We need to pay the rent. It's not your problem though, my dear, come and sit down."

"What can we do?" asked Polly, as their tension caused her own stomach to knot. "Will it be OK now you have let some go?"

"No," answered the Master, with a kind nod towards Polly, thanking her for her concern, "No, ' tis not so easy, lass. Theri don't stop coming, you see. All them pipes will be full again afore tomorrow. We need to get the barrels gone and sold. We need the boat to come, as normal, we need to ship the theri on the boat, down to Plymouth and fill up the empty barrels as we always do..."

Polly felt a little frustrated that the only solution given was that the boat should come and everything return to normal. Whatever the boat was and wherever it was, it had obviously not come for some reason and sitting and waiting did not seem the ideal solution. Tentatively she asked, "so do you know why the boat hasn't come and what will you do if it does not come?" Alba's sharp intake of breath made Polly realise she had asked a very sensitive question and been too forthright. She had sounded critical. "Lass," said Master Tremellin, "we don't know why the Doryty hasn't come. She comes each week early on Monday morning, but she has not been for near on four months now.....what will we do if she don't come? We shall have to move...leave pipes open and move. We have cousins in Bodmin..." his voice trailed away.

"Pa, we need to find out why she hasn't come though. We can't just give up," said Efrem, cautiously, not wanting to upset his father and supporting Polly's push to investigate and try to solve the problem.

"I don't like my cousins..." said the small Mabel, sitting on a stool at the end of the table.

"No, me neither, don't like," copied Carita with such a look of horror on her face that it made them all laugh. The two girls giggled at their joke and as the whole family laughed; the atmosphere lifted.

With a more hopeful and purposeful voice Master Tremellin indicated the map, "Lass, we know you are not from the boat, but you are from up there, from that world, from the house at end of the wood. Best we can do is try to find Doryty and the Cap'n. We have never been and we don't quite know where she comes from, apart from up the river. She might be up the river now, she might be down, she might be wrecked in Plymouth..."

"But we could look," Efrem said quickly to stop his father becoming sad again and losing his sense that something could be done. "We have a map which shows where the Cap'n lives and where Doryty is berthed. Look. Do you know how we can get there?"

The map was old and difficult to decipher, woods were coloured green and a huge river appeared to flow through the centre of the map. There were no villages marked or houses...her own house was not apparent at all, but various places in the woods were marked with blue flowers.

"What are these?" she asked.

"Where we live," answered Efrem, "each family of miners. And here, look, it's the daffodils," he said pointing to an area of yellow, "and this here, 'tis

Kitty, Wheal Kitty," his finger rested on a tiny, dark barrel shaped symbol. "This," he said, expansively, pointing to an inlet up the river, is where Doryty lies in harbour. We know, cos of the little flag here," and he pointed a grubby finger at a small symbol of a flag, lying at the head of a tributary. The flag seemed to have another barrel symbol, only this time in gold. "And to reach the harbour, we know there is a ladder, a long ladder, as once the Cap'n did tell us that the ladder needed mending. He took some wood from here, back up the river."

Polly tried to orientate the map. If she turned the map so that the yellow area indicating the daffodils was more or less pointing at them and made sure the family's house was lying to the south, she could easily see that the river was the same River Tamar which she walked beside most days, the wide river which ran through the bottom of the village, separating Devon and Cornwall. The inlet was just a little way upstream...but there was no scale to use to estimate exact distance.

"It's just up the river...we can go easily!" she said to them all. They reacted with looks of fear.

"We don't go out there," said Mistress Tremellin, "we know nothing about ...out there."

"I can take you," said Polly with enthusiasm.

"Nay," said Master Tremellin, "we don't want to be seen, we are no part of out there. We go to the river every Monday night and we load the barrels...we know the way to the loading weir and back....but we go in the dark. 'Tis how it is done, 'tis how it has always been done."

Polly again felt some frustration. From the map, the inlet with the boat appeared very close, so close she wondered why she had never stumbled on a boat full of treacle on her walks!

"I can take you one night?" she asked timidly, "should we do that?" The family all exchanged glances. It was clear she was suggesting something very unusual.

"No, no," said both Efrem's mother and father together, "we need to find the boat, maybe get a message to it? But I am not sure we can go..." Mistress Tremellin shook her head.

Polly's heart sank a little. The thought of finding some hidden harbour with a sailing boat was exciting and thrilling; the family's reluctance to explore was not easy to understand.

"So," she said, looking at Efrem, "so make more barrels? Sell the treacle somewhere else? How long have you got? Will the pipes explode soon?"

"Oh!" gasped Mistress Tremellin, glancing at the little girls to check they had not heard, "don't scare the girls, please Polly. We can make our own arrangements."

Aware she had offended Efrem's parents, Polly began to make excuses to leave. It was not her problem. When Mr Dominus and his mining company took over the wood, the treacle mine would be lost anyway. Maybe it would be good if they left sooner, rather than later...

"I am sorry," she smiled, "I could smell the theri, you see, and wondered if you were all OK."

"Aye," nodded Master Tremellin, "we will be. Doryty will come and we are making as many barrels as we can...all yards are full though...we will be fine. Thank you."

"Bye then," Polly said, waving at the girls, "Bye Efrem."

With a greyness filling her mind and a tiredness taking over her body, Polly shuffled back to the door in the tree and out into the darkening wood which was now cool with the evening. The chill air hit her forehead, waking her, and she lifted her face to the sky to breathe in the fresh, scented air.

"Polly," a voice called, "Polly, wait a moment." Efrem was walking towards her, pulling at his braces and pushing his arms into a woolly jacket. "Wait, Polly, I am as frustrated as you. Do wait."

Polly stopped and smiled, "Efrem, hi, don't worry. It's not my problem, but you are all so, so nice and so worried. I just thought we could find the boat. It can't be far away and you have a map," and she pointed towards the wide River Tamar which could just be glimpsed through the trees: a wide, murky brown, slow moving river.

"I know," said Efrem, sitting on a branch and dangling his legs down towards the little stream, "they are too scared though. They could be seen and we don't know what there is further up river. It scares us all."

"It's trees," Polly said, with a shrug, "trees and river…bit like here."

"mmm, maybe,"

"It is, Efrem. I don't get it. I don't. Why are you never seen anyway? And why can't you just let the treacle flow away until the boat comes again…your father seems to think it will come back, eventually. So let it flow away and wait…what's the big panic? If you let the theri flow, no one will be hurt…"

"Well, we need the money too, but I am not sure I am meant to talk to you," Efrem whispered cautiously.

"You live in my wood!"

"Our wood, always has been…"

"Well," said Polly, more quietly and holding onto Efrem's jacket to show she did not want to argue, "well, we might be losing it soon anyway…we can't afford to live here. "

"But it's the same with us, Polly! We need the Doryty to come so the pipes will stop clattering, but also to pay the rent…it's the same!"

"Yes, well, sort of," Polly replied, "we have to pay a mortgage." Efrem's expression told her he did not understand, "but yes, we also need to make money…and we are wondering how…" she stopped short of explaining about the mining company. "Who do you pay rent to, Efrem? I thought you, just lived there?"

"Oh we have to pay four sovereigns a month to the rent collector, the Roman rent collector."

"What?"

"The rent collector," he said, but Polly continued to look at him. " Since the days, many centuries ago, when we worked as slaves in the Roman copper and tin mines in Cornwall, they have let us mine for theri ourselves, if the mine is no good for metal, providing we pay rent. That's how it is. "

"So, a rent collector calls for your money, er, sovereigns."

"Aye," said Efrem," he does, but I don't see him. I don't like him. I'm not sure why. He is called Dominus, Dominus Magister."

Polly stared at him. Mr Dominus? A roman rent collector? Her face flushed.

"What does he look like, Efrem?"

"Oh, tall, wears black and looks ...nasty...like he does not care about us."

Polly stared ahead. The evening was closing in and there was not yet any moon to illuminate the pathways and trees. By screwing up her eyes tightly, she could see the mounds of newly dug soil, dumped uncaringly, as she thought, over a bank where the garlic plants grew. Beside the mounds were the exploratory holes dug by Mr Dominus and his mining engineers. Worlds seemed to be colliding in Polly's head and she could not explain it to herself, let alone the young boy sat beside her, glumly fiddling with the sleeve of his jacket.

"So, if you pay the...rent collector...what then?

"What then?" Efrem looked surprised by her question, "when we pay he goes away and we don't see him for another month. He goes away."

"He needs to, Efrem, he needs to go away. I can't explain, but he needs to go away."

"I know that, but we can't sell the theri."

Polly's face grew animated and she jumped down from the branch to stand in front of Efrem, "we have to sell it, Efrem. You need to sell it. I need Mr, er Dominus to go away too. We both need him to...clear off!" and she threw her arm wide as if dismissing the crow like man to the dark sky. "Bring me some theri Efrem and I will try to sell it. There are plenty of supermarkets," again Efrem did not seem to understand, "shops, Efrem, our shops, up here, why can't we try to sell it here?"

Efrem caught her mood, "I'll bring you a barrel. I'll leave it here tonight for you."

"Why don't you come and help sell it too?

"I, I can't be seen, Polly."

"Why not? I can see you perfectly well," she said with exasperation. " And for that matter, how do you hide yourselves from the village?"

"We, we are secretive," Efrem explained, swinging his legs quickly back and forward.

"Secretive?"

"Yes, we are secretive."

"Mmm, OK, what does that mean?" Polly was met with a silent shrug. "OK, well, leave a barrel here...not too big, Efrem. I think we need to get rid of your rent collector, I think it could help us both?"

With a determined nod of the head, smile and new energy, Efrem, jumped down from the tree and turned to go home; Polly, cautiously, in the gloomy dark, picked her way along the path to her home.

Secretive? She thought. That explains nothing! She peered back along the path towards the tree; a soft mist had begun to settle over the stream and she felt she was looking into a grey, gently moving cloud. She knew Efrem was there, but however hard she looked, she could only see black and grey; the mist distorted her vision and perception. It made her feel alone in a damp, soft cushion of cloud. She could not see the tree, the branch where they had sat...or Efrem.

Chapter Six

"The mining engineers were very optimistic about their first results," said Polly's father over breakfast.

"What does that mean?" asked Polly.

"Well, they think there could still be copper here. They are coming back tomorrow to do more tests." No one smiled. It was not entirely good news: they wanted to stay in their home and the sale of the wood made that a possibility, but they would lose the wood.

"Who is Mr Dominus, anyway?" asked Polly with a mouthful of porridge, "why our wood?"

"Because, Polly," replied her father, "there used to be considerable mining here, so it's a very likely place to find copper."

"Yes, there used to be flower farms and apple orchards too!"

"Yes, I know," her father sighed, "but they don't pay the mortgage. You know this."

"Yes, I expect you don't care that the deer will be chased off...and the flowers killed...and the badgers!"

"Polly, if we could..." Polly scowled at her parents and, even though she knew it was not their fault, stormed out of the room. She wanted them to feel guilty for her loss.

The return visit of the engineers forced Polly to think hard about how to sell the theri herself. Mr Dominus, or Dominus Magister, needed to be paid. If he was receiving regular rent again, surely he would be satisfied and leave them all alone? It did not secure their future, but it was a step in the right direction and the wood might be saved. Polly made her way to the barn, checked that the barrel of theri was safe under the hay bales and rang the local supermarket.

"The manager please," she asked.

"Who is calling?"

"Po..Miss Evans," she stammered, "I need to speak to the manager please."

After a few minutes of music a man's voice came on the phone, "good afternoon, how may I help you?"

"I am a producer of treacle and wondered if you would like to buy it," Polly stammered, speaking very quickly.

"Treacle?"

"The black, thick treacle, like you put in Christmas puddings, do you know what I mean?"

"Yes, Miss Evans, I do. We don't sell a great deal, but we do have a small producers' day soon, if I can send you details do come along. You would need to be able to tell us how much you could deliver and when. We are keen to support local business, you know. Our health and safety people would need to inspect the premises of course...that is if we like the product. "

"Inspect...ah, of course..."

"Can I take the name of the business and some information? You can register interest on line or we can arrange a meeting with my secretary? Tomorrow?"

"Oh, I have scho...no...I am afraid I can't make tomorrow. I have a...a...meeting, with barrel makers."

"Barrels? Of course, everything we sell would need to be in uniform glass, sterilised bottles and..."

"Yes, yes, well thank you. I'll be in touch..."

"Miss Evans, your E mail?" but Polly had turned off her phone and with a flushed, burning face lay back on the sweet-smelling hay. This was too difficult; maybe people just did not buy the stuff!

Later that afternoon, Polly took a small jar of black, sticky treacle, scooped from the barrel, to her mother in the kitchen. "Mum, a friend gave me this.

Can you use it? I wondered if we could make a cake or something."

"Well, it's nice you are talking to us now, Poll. We don't want to sell the wood or the house, Polly, you know that, and we will make sure we move somewhere we all like..." Polly's mother tried to put her arms around her daughter, but Polly shrugged her away.

"I know Mum, sorry. But, can you use this?"

"What is it, there's no label?" asked Polly's mother holding the jar up to the light.

"It's treacle, Mum. Shall we cook something? See if it's nice? "

"Well, who gave it to you? Is it within the sell by date? I haven't cooked with treacle for years, to be honest. I think your Gran used to make something: flapjacks or was it gingerbread men?"

"Oh it's very fresh...the, um, new girl gave it to me...for you!"

"We could try it, Poll," said her mother sniffing the jar, "it smells lovely, sort of sweet and earthy."

"I know, taste it Mum. I'll look on the internet for recipes."

Polly's Mum dipped one finger in the thick syrup and, sniffing it first, tasted it. "Oh it's nice, Polly, not too sweet...but what a strange thing to give you."

"I have a recipe," called Polly, from behind the lap top, ignoring her mother's disquiet, "called Parkin...soft and sticky cake...shall we?"

The parkin was such a success, so soft and sticky that she printed off the recipe and took it to Mistress Tremellin, just before dusk that evening.

"There's a jumble sale in the village next week. Do you think you could make this? Quite a lot? I can then sell it and we should make loads of money! What do you think?"

Mistress Tremellin was reading the recipe carefully and noting down the many things she did not have, "I have heard of ginger, but I don't have any...and flour...we would need a lot of flour Polly."

"I'll bring that," she said, deleting it from the list and calculating how far the money in her purse would stretch, "do you have enough cake tins or trays?"

"I can borrow, yes, we have plenty. Well, Polly," Mistress Tremellin smiled and clasped Polly's hand; "you have come up with a plan. We will use as much treacle as we can and are you sure you can sell the cakes?"

"Oh yes, it's just delicious. I would have brought you some, but Dad ate it all!" she laughed.

A week later, in the chilly garage of a nearby house, the parkin was displayed in dark, glistening chunks on white plates. Old clothes and broken plastic toys covered other tables and were being picked over by people from the village, keen to find anything worth buying and therefore donate to the charity. Polly had told her mother she was "selling the cakes for a friend" and was delighted with the queue waiting to buy a square of parkin at 50 pence each. Her empty yoghurt pot was virtually full of silver coins.

An old lady approached the table. It was Mrs Perkins, who had worked on the daffodil farm, which had thrived before the woodland covered the ground. She had been a young girl when she had worked on the farm and had told Polly of the difficulty in picking daffodils on such a slope. She told her how the daffodils had to be picked when the bud was still tightly closed and how the green buds were transported to Plymouth by boat and then to Covent Garden by train, to reach the flower stalls of London within a day.

"This is very tasty, Polly, well done," she said biting into a large, square of sweet-smelling cake, "I don't know when I last saw parkin for sale."

"Thank you, Mrs Perkins, but a friend made it, not me."

"Still, it's very soft and such a lovely taste..."

"Oh that's probably the treacle," Polly blurted, "mm, yes, it could be the treacle used...or the ginger?"

"Treacle?" asked Mrs Perkins and her eyes met Polly's. Polly tried to look away, but Mrs Perkins maintained her gaze and her eyes, which were still a deep blue, even though they were surrounded by rather wrinkly skin and tended to water, seemed to be asking Polly a question.

"Treacle, Polly," she said, quietly, taking another bite, "I remember this variety, what is it called?"

Polly could not reply and looking deep into the old lady's eyes, she merely shook her head, "no name, Mrs Perkins, it doesn't have a name..."

Mrs Perkins took two pound-coins from her purse and dropped them into the yoghurt pot, "there, I have now paid for the lot. Come and sit with me over there," she pointed with her stick towards a garden chair, set back from the sale, under a willow tree which was just beginning to show a springtime glimmer of bright green on the tips of each branch.

"So," she said, as Polly sat nervously beside her, "tell me about treacle."

"I think it comes in jars," said Polly, but Mrs Perkins interrupted her. Again, she seemed to look deeply into Polly's eyes and her blue eyes twinkled with expectation.

"You know, don't you? "

"Know, er, what? Mrs Perkins?"

"What if I say theri," she whispered, her face turned towards the tree and away from the few remaining villagers looking for a bargain.

"What?" said Polly, loudly, blushing red.

"Theri, you have used theri. Nothing tastes quite the same." There was a long moment as they both looked at each other, and slowly smiled.

"Polly. How did you get it? I have never seen it, beyond, beyond..."

"The wood."

"Yes, Polly, the wood. Do tell me, is everything alright? Don't worry about telling me. No one knows about the miners, but me. Only me." She lowered her voice. "I once met a young lad, gathering herbs or such like, many, many years ago, when I was working in the field, by the stream. Tremellin, he was called..." she looked away, towards the bright sun. "He could hide himself using nature you know, the sun, the mist and fog...but I could see him, most of the time. Or hear him...he wasn't very careful," she laughed," He must be about sixty by now!"

"That must be Master Tremellin," smiled Polly excitedly, enjoying the relief of speaking to someone who knew about the treacle mine, "must be...how amazing! I thought I was the only one who knew. Do others know too?" asked Polly looking at the villagers on the other side of the garden.

"Oh no, Polly. Only me," whispered Mrs Perkins.

"But why not? Others might have seen them too?"

"Most people choose not to look or listen to what is around them. I do and you do too. I can tell that. I have thought about this a great deal over the years, Polly and I believe people don't see them for two reasons, firstly because the miners are secretive and secondly because people choose not to look."

"Amazing," repeated Polly, looking in wonder at the old lady sat beside her, "but what does secretive mean? They always tell me they are…secretive."

"Well, he, the Tremellin lad, told me that they purposefully use nature to help hide themselves. Anyone can do it, if you know how. For example, they know that the bright sun dazzles people, so if you position yourself carefully, you can't be seen."

"Yes, Efrem. Master Tremellin's son, he did that. I couldn't look into the sun, so I couldn't see him. It was all just glare and brightness. But he kept talking, so I knew he was there!" she laughed.

"Sounds like the lad I met. I wonder if it was his father…how wonderful."

"How else do they hide?" asked Polly urgently, delighting in the fact she could talk about her strange, secretive friends, "is it just the sun they use?"

"As I said, they use nature. They use mist and fog. The river is coated in fog most nights, you know that, and it distorts the vision of anyone looking into it, especially if you have a torch or car headlights. Nothing looks real, so it's easy to hide. Fog… sort of distorts perception. They can hide, as people choose not to look too closely. They blame the unreal shadows on the fog, on their lights reflecting back on them and I expect they just think about getting home for their tea, out of the gloom."

"And fog dampens noise, doesn't it?" said Polly, thinking about how the miners move the barrels through the village, without being heard, "fog softens noise, doesn't it? It distorts sound?"

"Yes," smiled Mrs Perkins, "ideal for covering the sound of wheelbarrows laden with barrels of sweetness..." and she winked.

"You have seen that?" asked Polly, grasping the old lady's arm.

"Of course. But, before all of that, tell me. Why are you selling cake that is brimming with delicious theri? Is there a problem? Her face became serious, "are those sweet, secretive folk well?"

In whispers Polly told Mrs Perkins about the clattering which threatened to explode the pipes and the homes of the miners. She told her about the boat not coming and the fact that there was so much treacle, but none of it was being sold so there was no money to pay the rent.

"He's called Dominus Magister, and," she lowered her voice even more, "there is a man, a real man in our world, called Mr Dominus who is looking at turning the wood into one huge, horrible, dirty mine...he can't be the same person, can he?" She said it very tentatively, as if dipping her toe into a cold sea.

"It can, Polly. It can. I know the miners always had to pay rent for the treacle mine and I know that they paid someone who wasn't a miner. It sounded like he crossed over into our world, if you can understand. Sounds like him, or his descendant."

They both looked anxiously at each other.

"What can we do?" asked Polly.

"Let me think," replied the old lady, "why not come and see me tomorrow afternoon, after school. Bring theri and the recipe...and remember, they don't want to be known or seen. "

"Don't worry, I can be as secretive as them," smiled Polly, putting her finger to her lips.

Chapter Seven

Polly sat down at Mrs Perkin's kitchen table. There was a pot of tea and chocolate biscuits, neatly laid out in a circle on a plate. On the wall were some pictures of a much younger Mrs Perkins with boxes of daffodils, bunched with string and still in bud, spread around her. Other young women and some children sat on boxes and smiled, in muffled black and white, at the camera.

"I have a friend, Polly, who bakes cakes for events. Wedding cakes, tea parties, birthdays. She would buy some theri. I talked her into a barrel!"

"I think that is brilliant! We need to sell as much as we can, I only made three pounds at the sale..." replied Polly, hoping it would be enough to pay the rent and see the back of Mr Dominus. "But will it stop the clattering? How much can she use? I presume we need to sell loads of barrels, not just one? Although it is an excellent idea!" she added with a smile.

"She has contacts, dear, suppliers and the like. If people like it, we could start selling more. It's a start, don't you think?"

"So, can you fetch the treacle?" Mrs Perkins looked excited and her blue eyes danced.

"I will go and see the family tonight. How can we transport the treacle, won't it be really heavy?"

"Well," said Mrs Perkins, who did look quite frail and very old in Polly's eyes, "I will book a taxi, travel to the train station and then catch the train. There are still porters on stations aren't there? I'll shout for one! Then a taxi the other end," she grasped her hands together in excitement, "what an adventure!"

"Won't people ask what is in the barrel?" asked Polly, cautiously.

"Thought of that! I'm going to say it's beer!" and Mrs Perkins giggled like the young teenager she once was, "If they ask more, I'll just say it's none of their business!"

Polly made her way along the woodland path to visit the miners. The daffodil shoots were now at knee height and some very brave, early primroses were blooming, shining yellow against the still wet, dark soil. She stopped to pick a few as a present for Efrem's mother and placing her hand on the ground, she was shocked to feel the soil tremble. Standing very still, she thought she could feel the ground under her feet shake slightly. Was she imagining it? Leaving the primroses unpicked Polly ran to the tree and pushed open the heavy door. Immediately she heard the booming and banging of the pipes as they crashed together, the floor of the corridor was trembling and at first Polly wanted to run home, but she took a deep breath and continued to the kitchen door. Inside the kitchen the noise was even louder and she felt each thud deep in her stomach.

The kitchen seemed smaller and it was only after a few moments that Polly realised each wall was obscured by barrels, stacked to the ceiling. Above the thudding of the pipes, the barrels were softly clinking together, like a harmony in a church choir. Mistress Tremellin and the younger girls were stood, with their hands grasping the edge of the table and looking with fear at the walls.

"It's the worst yet, Polly, be careful," shouted Mistress Tremellin, "the rest are all down below. The more there are to find out which pipe is blocked, the better."

Polly moved to stand next to her and she mimicked her stance, holding onto the table. A glass jar containing stewed apples fell from a high shelf and smashed on the floor; the girls screamed and ran to stand even closer to their mother. Eventually, there was a high pitched, metallic scream which made them all grit their teeth and grimace; the shriek of metal sliced the air and then...it was silent. Polly could hear the gasping, quick breathing of the family and realised that she too was panting, as if she had run a race.

"It's over," said Efrem's mother, pulling the children away from the shattered glass, "it's all fine, do not worry. Efrem and your father have stopped it. Polly, do sit down, it's done."

The girls appeared from behind their mother and with wide eyes scanned each corner of the room, checking that the clattering had stopped; with their eyes still fixed on the walls, they cautiously sat down while their mother picked up glass with her hand wrapped in a rag.

"I'll make a warm drink for us and the others. I still have ginger," she said over her shoulder, as the door at the back of the kitchen opened, bringing with it a blast of heat and smell of sweetness mixed with oil.

Master Tremellin, Efrem and Alba walked slowly into the room; Alba was clutching her hand.

"What have you done?" asked her mother rushing to her side and gently opening her hand.

"She got it stuck between a crowbar and the pipe, Marfa," said the Master, "she's being so brave," he put his arm around his daughter. Efrem smiled, sadly, at Polly.

Alba's hand was very bloody and her two middle fingers seem to bend the wrong way.

"Oh," said Polly, with shock, when she saw her hand.

"'Tis, fine," said Mistress Tremellin, smiling reassuringly at Alba and calmly leading her to the sink to wash away the grime and blood. Alba was sobbing very quietly and staring at her hand.

“”We will wash it, Alba, and then bind those fingers tightly, here drink this water.” Holding back her own shock, Mistress Tremellin quietly washed the hand and murmured reassuring nonsense to her daughter.

“I’ll take her to see Old Claudia, she has some lovely herbs and lotions which will sort this out,” said Mistress Tremellin, putting a blue cape around the shoulders of her daughter and untying her apron. She led her daughter out into the corridor, maintaining her false cheeriness all the while.

“The fingers?” whispered Polly to the shocked family.

“They’ll need to be re-set, in the right position,” said Master Tremellin, with anger in his voice. “We need to sell and we need the boat to come...or we should leave. I’m not having my children hurt! I can’t let this continue. ”

Polly could see that he was furious; his eyes were brimming with tears and the little girls both began to cry.

Efrem sat heavily at the table, his grimy face was sad and worried.

“It’s going to hurt her, isn’t it Pa?” he asked, looking up at his father.

“Aye, it is,” he replied and then, not wanting to upset the younger girls, he added, “but she will be fine. A few weeks and she will be just fine again.

Come here," he said to the girls, who climbed into his lap.

"But we are not going to be fine, are we Pater?" said Efrem, so quietly the girls did not notice.

"I don't know, my lad. We need to find the boat. I think we will have to look for the boat and the Cap'n. We need to go into the forest and search. It's no good just sitting here, waiting. It's no good just waiting and trying to divert the theri. It's no good being scared. It's no good having your own children hurt."

Polly handed Master Tremellin and Efrem warm mugs of a gingery tea.

"Gratias," they murmured. She then, very tentatively told them how she could sell one barrel for them, if that would help.

"Anything would help," said Efrem, swinging his arm wide to point at the barrels stacked up every wall.

"But you would have to help me deliver it to Mrs Perkins, in the village, Efrem."

"Well, Pa, I can if it's dark, can't I?" asked Efrem.

"Aye, lad. Tonight it will be cold, there will be a good mist. Be careful and take the wheelbarrow...go before the moon comes up." He turned to Polly, "thank you for this. Some sovereigns to pay the rent collector will be very welcome, thank you." With his sad eyes turned towards the door, watching for the return of his eldest daughter, he snuggled the little girls closer.

It was arranged for Efrem to be outside Polly's door with a wheelbarrow and a barrel before the moon came up. Polly was not sure what time this meant, so watched from her window. The night was dark and even though it was the start of Spring, the cold air had created a foggy mist hanging over the stream and her garden.

Polly stared into the mist and just as Mrs Perkins had explained, she saw darker shadows which could not be explained. The garden chair? The bird table? The shine on the wheel of a wheelbarrow? The mist lightened the dark but did not make it any easier to see through the grey froth.

Something was moving slowly down the track; slipping in and out of the misty obscurity and quietly creeping down the stairs she let herself out the back door.

"Efrem?" she whispered.

"Aye, I'm here," he replied and though she could still see a shine from the barrel or wheelbarrow, she could not see him at all.

"Follow me," she whispered, "If you can see me."

"I can see you clearly, can you see me?"

"Not at all!"

"Good, I'll follow."

Efrem sounded nervous and he followed Polly very slowly.

"What are you doing?" she hissed, "why are you so slow?"

"Being careful," he replied, "never been this way before. I've been to the weir, never this way…what is that? Efrem jumped slightly and Polly saw his white face for the first time; he was wearing a dark coat and a black or dark brown cap was pulled low over his forehead.

"It's a cat, don't worry, Efrem," she said, as a large ginger cat leapt a garden wall. She reached to touch his arm, however, this only made him jump again and the barrel clattered softly in the wheelbarrow. Polly could just see that it was wrapped in blankets and rags, presumably to lessen any chance of noise.

"Just, just follow, Efrem. You are making me nervous."

They reached Mrs Perkins' cottage and walked down the garden path. Polly knocked gently on the door and it was opened immediately.

"Well Done, Polly," the old lady said looking down at the girl and the barrow, "you have done well, bringing it on your own. We need to lift it out though, how will..."

"Efrem helped me, Mrs Perkins, he..." and she turned around but there was only the barrow and its cushioned load to be seen.

"Oh," said Mrs Perkins and she stepped back from the doorway, out of the light, "Efrem, can you help lift it out for us?" she called into the darkness, the nothingness.

There was silence for a few long moments.

"Yes," came a muffled response and a figure emerged from the dark shadows and lifted the barrel from the barrow. "Where?" asked the shadow.

"Just inside the porch here, dear, I have left the light on so you can see where to put it," replied Mrs Perkins, "I'll keep back."

Efrem placed the barrel on the slate floor and quickly began to turn away, he then stopped and pulling his cap low over his face he said, "thank you."

"I hope it helps, Efrem. I met your father years ago, you know," Mrs Perkins said gently.

"Did you?" Efrem slowly raised his head and looked Mrs Perkins fully in the face, their eyes met, two sets of blue eyes stared deep into each other, "did you?" he asked again.

"I did and it's a pleasure to meet you too," replied Mrs Perkins, barely speaking above a whisper. She held out her hand and with their eyes still locked,

Efrem removed his cap, took her hand and shook it, a little clumsily, and with a shy smile said clearly and loudly, "thank you, Mrs Perkins."

Polly had not managed to persuade her parents that she needed a trip to Plymouth and was old enough to go with friends.

"No, Polly, I don't want you on the train on your own," her father had said.

"I won't be on my own, Dad; I'll be with friends and..."

"I am quite happy to take you all into town in the car. I'll find something to do while you shop and then we can all meet for lunch."

"Dad..." Polly moaned.

"You can't go on your own, Polly. Not yet."

So Mrs Perkins had caught the train alone, with her barrel of beer, and travelled into Plymouth for the first time in nearly ten years. She enjoyed every second of her adventure and told Polly ten times about how she had to convince a porter at the station that the barrel needed to travel with her, as she was attending a wedding and had brewed the beer herself as a present.

"First thing I thought of," she laughed, as Polly ate biscuits and drank tea in Mrs Perkins' cottage, "first thing I thought of! They need my beer at the wedding, I said. Of course, he thought I was mad."

Polly laughed, "so you delivered it safely?"

"Oh yes, at the bakery, my friend sent out a baker to carry it. He was built like a wrestler, great muscular arms, from kneading bread I suppose. Anyway, here it is," and she placed six blue five-pound notes on the table and five one pound coins. " I also have a cake for the family, for poor Alba," she opened a cardboard box and showed Polly a beautiful sponge strawberry cake, decorated with swirls of cream and quartered berries. "If I put the money in an envelope, could you carry the box to the tree?"

"Of course, well done, Mrs Perkins! They will love the cake," said Polly and she dropped the envelope into the box, beside the cake.

"Wouldn't you like to come too? No one will see us?"

"I had such a good day, my dear, but I am so tired…also, if I remember, the path through your wood is not very easy going. I'm not as young as I used to be, Polly, when I could run from home to the daffodil field as quick as…as quick as …"

"a rabbit being chased!"

"Yes," Mrs Perkins laughed, "that quick. No, do take the cake and money and my love. I have had enough adventure today! Do tell them that if Alba needs anything for her poor hand, they must say."

"I will," said Polly and she bent to kiss the old lady on her stubbly cheek.

Polly returned to her home for the evening meal and found it hard to think of a reason why she needed to go out again. It was a chilly, frosty evening and there was a fire burning cosily in the hearth.

"I…I'll shut in the chickens for you, Dad," she said.

"Oh don't worry. It's cold. You stay inside," he replied.

"Oh, but I need…an egg for DT tomorrow."

"I have some in the kitchen, Polly," muttered her mother who was looking through leaflets from estate agents.

"It…it needs to be fresh, so I'll just go and see if they have laid a fresh one…" and she got up to leave before they could argue.

"The ones in the kitchen are fresh, but go and look if you want to," her mother replied, distracted by the leaflets.

"Yes, needs to be very, very fresh," Polly called over her shoulder as she picked up the box from its hiding place underneath the coats and using a torch, made her way towards the dark, quiet wood.

It felt a little eerie and Polly was glad to reach the miner's tree. She pushed open the door in the tree and was relieved that there was no clattering, thudding or shaking.

The family were sat around the table eating soup and the sweet smell of garlic, treacle and cream made Polly's mouth water. Alba's hand was wrapped in a snowy white bandage and her whole arm was supported by a bright blue sling, which looked a great deal like Mistress Tremellin's head scarf. Alba smiled.

"How are you, Alba?" Polly asked,

"Oh it's better every day. Thank you. I won't rush to help with the pipes next time though!" she said with a kind smile.

"Aye, you won't," said Master Tremellin, pointing his spoon at her, "one injury is more than enough."

Polly had little time as she was only meant to be shutting the door on the roosting chickens. "I have to rush, but here," she said, as if making a grand announcement, "the money for the barrel and Mrs Perkins has sent you a cake!" The little girls lifted the lid together and gasped at the extravagant cake, "strawberries!" they both said together.

"Strawberries," said Mistress Tremellin, leaving her seat to look, "it's not the time of year for strawberries, how..."

"In our shops, we can always get strawberries," Polly beamed.

"They are ten times bigger than the ones in the wood," said Mistress Tremellin in wonder.

"The money is in the envelope," said Polly, again speaking as if she was announcing an award winner. " I have to run home, but we do hope it helps!"

The family smiled at her and Polly felt as if she had won a medal or an award on Prize Day.

"Gratias Tibi," said Master Tremellin.

"Thank you," they all said together.

"And for the cake!" said Mabel, sticking a finger into the cream and holding it up for all to see.

Another week passed before Polly could again go to visit the miners in the wood. The evenings were slowly lengthening, but it was hard to find reasons to leave the house in the dark. Mr Dominus had apparently visited again, with more engineers, digging more holes, but Polly had been at school and managed, therefore, to avoid seeing him. She did wonder why he was still interested and if the money from the barrel had not been enough for him. Scientists had also visited, concerned about the loss of historic daffodils, should the wood become a mine again. As there were fewer daffodils each year, they had told Polly's mother that they had no grounds to oppose the mining venture.

It was Saturday, late afternoon before the routine of school and home released her so she could run along the path, now beginning to turn green with fresh moss and new leaves, and ask the Tremellins if they had managed to pay the rent and satisfy Mr Dominus. There was a slight trembling in the ground as she made her way along the tunnel from the door to the kitchen. Efrem and his father were not in the room, Alba sat in her father's chair, cradling her arm and the girls sat squashed together in a mass of blue cloth and black curls, reading a very old, tattered book with a dormouse on the cover. Mistress Tremellin was lighting the fire.

"Has there been more clattering?" asked Polly, placing her hand on the floor to feel the soft tremble.

"Yes, Polly, yes. But it has stopped now and I expect the others will be back soon, safe and sound," she glanced anxiously at Alba as she spoke.

"The cake was delicious," said Mabel and she licked her lips in memory, making a smacking, sticky sound.

"Delicious," echoed her sister, Carita, "Gratias," she added, noticing her mother's scowl.

"Yes, girls. Be polite please," she said firmly, "thank you Polly, we all enjoyed it very much. Such strawberries! We have saved you some."

"It was from Mrs Perkins, really," she replied, "but thank you. But, the rent collector, Dominus Magister," she said carefully, trying to say his name correctly, "have we managed to get rid of him for a while?" In Polly's head she could visualise the newly dug holes she had just run past, the puddle of oil reflecting the moon in unnatural, fluorescent swirling colours, the new green shoots trodden underfoot on the path and the white, sprouting daffodil bulbs unearthed and flung on the heaps of soil like unwanted rubbish. "Have we managed to pay him off for a while? Have we got rid of him?"

There was no answer and the family were looking at her strangely as if they did not quite understand.

"Was it enough money for him? At least for a while?" she pursued, smiling, but Alba and her mother exchanged embarrassed glances. The girls turned back to their story book.

"Did you manage to pay the rent?" Polly asked, fervently trying to rephrase her question. She looked from Mistress Tremellin to Alba, seeking an answer and her eye caught something glittering around Alba's neck. She was wearing a necklace and the pendant appeared to be made from a one pound coin. A hole had been drilled in the coin to allow for the blue ribbon to pass through. Polly did not understand.

"The money, for the barrel...was it enough rent?" she asked again, noticing that both the little girls had similar necklaces.

"The rent?" Mistress Tremellin said softly, catching something of Polly's anxiety, "we pay the rent in sovereigns. There were no sovereigns in the box. We looked." Mistress Tremellin smiled warmly, but with embarrassment; she did not want to upset Polly and did not quite understand her questions.

"There was money," said Polly, quietly, "there was quite a lot of money." Polly felt as if a heavy, grey blanket had been dropped on her. She stood still, looking at Mistress Tremellin incomprehensibly.

"No dear. No money, but a glorious cake, we did enjoy it so much," she turned to the fire, "just let me light the fire and you must have a piece." Mistress Tremellin struck a flint hard to create a spark and then lit a small, bluish piece of paper, blowing softly on the speck of gold to create a good, strong flame; she then slowly bent forward to place the burning paper on top of a small mound of crumpled, blue, five-pound notes.

"There," she said, "we'll have a lovely fire in no time."

Chapter Eight

"They burnt the money!" cried Polly, as she sat, deflated, in Mrs Perkins' kitchen, "they made necklaces out of the coins and just burnt the money."

Mrs Perkins sat down heavily in the chair opposite; her eyes were full of shock and disbelief. She said nothing.

" Sovereigns," Mistress Tremellin said, she said there were no sovereigns," Polly muttered, wiping her nose on her sleeve and sniffing loudly.

"Sovereigns?" Mrs Perkins looked up, "oh I see! How stupid I was. Oh I am so sorry, Polly."

"For what? We both tried really hard and ...they burnt it!"

"No, Polly. Don't blame them. It's my fault," the old lady patted Polly's hand and spoke with conviction, "it's my fault for being so vain and silly. Thinking I could help! What an old fool I am..."

"What?"

"They pay their rent in sovereigns, Polly. Old fashioned coins. I expect they had no idea what the money was...no idea at all."

"But...but Mr Dominus, or Dominus Magister whatever his name is, he might have accepted the money anyway. It still could have been enough!"

"But they didn't know that, Polly. They had no idea they were throwing away anything of value. No, don't mention anything to them. It's my fault entirely."

"No," Polly sniffed and looked kindly up at the old lady, "it's my fault too. I am the one who has heard them talk about sovereigns. I never thought..."

The pair fell quiet and both sighed deeply. "So, if we can't help by giving them money for the treacle, I don't think we can do anything. We can't stop the clattering," Polly sighed again, "so I expect they will have to move and so will I. The wood will become a mine, that's it!" and she pulled her arm across her face, wiping tears on her sleeve and sniffing loudly.

"Here," Mrs Perkins handed her a tissue, "use this. If we can't sell the theri, then the only thing to do is to find the boat, so they can sell it themselves...for sovereigns. "

"Do you know where it could be and why it might have stopped coming?"

"No, but they need to find out. You need to convince them to look. They must leave the wood."

"They are so scared of leaving the wood. Even coming in the village seems terrifying to them!" Polly said, remembering Efrem's nerves.

"They will need to venture upstream and look. I'm too old, but you need to try to convince them, don't you think?"

"Oh I want Mr Dominus to go away and leave us all alone and I want the clattering to stop. It's just getting more and more dangerous for them!"

"I know, Polly. Poor Alba...and there will be more accidents if this continues."

It was not hard for Polly to persuade the miners that they needed to look for the boat. The clattering was happening more often and they had now stopped trying to divert the flow of treacle into different pipes; since Alba's accident the whole community decided that the safest reaction to any blocked and bulging pipe was to open the huge cog wheels and let the dark sweetness pour out into the soil and be lost.

The map was brought out again and the family tried to pin point their house, the stream, the larger River Tamar and the harbour, where they hoped Doryty was lying.

"I can go," said Polly looking at their pale, nervous faces, "I have walked in those woods many, many times."

"Thank you," said Efrem's father, "I don't think we should send too many people...not on the first trip. Not until we know what is out there."

'Trees,' thought Polly in her head, "so I'll go," she said aloud, "I'll go and look and report back."

"I'll go with you," said Efrem, "I have already been into the village and no one saw us. We know how to be quiet, Pater. We can take a lantern and go careful."

"And me! Me!" shouted the girls, although Alba stayed quiet.

"If you go at night and take great care..." said Master Tremellin with a look of great concern.

"And take some warm soup," said Efrem's mother, pulling at her hair.

"And a great big stick!" shouted Mabel, breaking the tension; the family laughed.

So the plan was made.

Chapter Nine

The plan was for Polly and Efrem to search upstream, at night, armed with the map, a lantern for Efrem and a strong torch for Polly, some provisions and lots of questions to ask the Captain of the Doryty.

Efrem had met the rather surly, capable and efficient Captain before, when they loaded full barrels onto the boat on Monday nights. On these occasions, the miners rolled many, many barrels, slurping with treacle, through the tracks in the wood, past Polly's house, through the sleeping village to a small weir on the River Tamar. They made their way through the village at the darkest point of night, slipping in and out of mist, with the barrels swaddled in rags and towels. Villagers thought the weir and its decrepit wooden jetty were merely ruins, long deserted by the hard working and down trodden copper miners, who had mined in the valley over one hundred years ago. No one could see or notice that the spikey, broken jetty had been piled high with barrels, rope and miners clad in blue, each and every Monday evening, as they waited for the Doryty to sail around the bend...unless the moon was full and the light too bright. No one saw the pulling and throwing of ropes, or the Doryty moor alongside for half an hour as the miners unloaded the hold of empty barrels to be pushed back up the hill, and carried full, slightly sticky barrels below deck. The Doryty had a steam engine, but it was seldom used as it was noisy and left behind the smell of coal, like a sign that they had been there; when under sail, she left no trace.

The Captain would pay them the sovereigns earned the previous week, grunt a little at each miner, call his collie dog on board, who excitedly greeted each person and jumped from the boat to the land in swirls of joy, always judging it just right to avoid falling into the black water. Then the boat would sail away and the miners begin to push, pull and carry the empty barrels back up the hill, through the sleeping village and back to the treacle mines. Some mining families had small trailers, made of wood and metal, which they over loaded and pulled behind them, being careful to avoid bumps and stones in the road, some carried the barrels on their shoulders with their heads bent forward and some had wheelbarrows which could carry two or even three carefully balanced barrels. Not all families entered their homes through Efrem's wood, some lived further away and turned up other tracks to left and right, waving silent goodbyes. It was mainly those families who chose to use trailers, if they possibly could. Each family had their name carved into the barrels and some were painted bright colours, almost as if the children had been let loose with a paint box. The Tremellin barrels had their name carved around the top and four pale daffodils painted below...one for each child, Efrem explained.

They left no tracks.

Efrem was a little worried about meeting with the Captain and venturing upstream through another, larger forest area. Polly had walked by the river many times and found it hard to understand his fear. It was home to her, however, she seldom, if ever, had walked into the forest at night.

Polly had set her alarm for 1 am and met Efrem by her back door. Even though the meeting was planned, she was thoroughly shocked to see him in her world, by her door, his heavy boots planted sturdily beside a pot of herbs and the recycling bin, and it took her a while to adjust to the strange merging of worlds. He was stood awkwardly near the door, a thick, dark coloured jacket covering his normal breeches, his black cap pulled low over his face and holding a bag and an unlit lantern.

She flicked on her torch and, picking up a ruck sac said, "Come on then, let's go." He stood still, looking with some nervousness at the bright torch.

"Too bright, lass, I can't see. We don't make lanterns like that..."

She turned off the bright torch and they soon found that the moonlight was all they needed to find their way into the forest which covers the Cornish bank of the river for some miles. It was a cold night; spring had come to their wood and daffodils were close to opening, but the forest of conifers was too dark for there to be any flowers or warmth. The track was initially broad and rutted from the heavy forestry vehicles, but, after a mile it became a narrow path only frequented by dog walkers and the forest animals of deer, badger and fox. Although the ground was covered in pine needles and was soft underfoot, fallen branches made it difficult to walk at any speed. Moonlight played with the shadows and both children, although they were trying to be brave for each other, occasionally looked over their shoulder or behind them, as a shadow seemed to draw breath and move.

The map led them to some stone mine buildings, ruins of huts and an old adit[1] which Polly had seen many times, but never been near. "There can be huge drops Polly, don't go near the entrance," her mother would say. As the map seemed to tell them

---

[1] A horizontal passage leading into a mine for the purposes of access or drainage.

to leave the known path here and venture towards the adit, Polly was instantly cautious. “It’s too dangerous to go in there Efrem. It’s a tunnel, an old mining tunnel and there could be land slips, shafts…anything. You haven’t been here before, remember! I have seen that entrance many times and my mother won’t ever let us near.”

“I know, but ‘tis strange that the map shows this way…” he said quietly, leaving Polly and walking with great care towards the low tunnel, where all he could see was treacle blackness and all he could hear was water dropping from the roof onto stone like an old clock ticking. The entrance to the adit, or tunnel, was covered in soft moss, so thick it formed a wet cushion and Efrem rested his forehead on the top of the entrance to peer into the darkness. “Can’t see nothing,” he whispered. Strange, how their surroundings made them whisper, as if afraid something in the forest would hear.

“Stay there; don’t go further in, I’m coming over,” replied Polly softly, as she made her way over rubble, broken branches and ruined walls to reach him. They both leaned their foreheads on the moss and peered. The blurriness on the edge of their vision grew clearer and as their eyes grew accustomed to the darkness, they both saw, almost simultaneously, a doorway, built into the right-hand side of the tunnel. It was within reach and Polly marvelled that in every walk she had ever had, to this place, this very place, she had not seen the doorway. It was slightly hidden by the curve of the entrance and moss did obscure the detail, but it was clearly there. Any blurriness of sight was gone. The ground before the door looked solid stone and they would not have to venture into the tunnel to reach the handle...so, without a word they stepped forward and reached for the cold, wet iron handle. To their surprise, it turned easily and the wooden door swung open.

On the other side they found themselves standing at the top of a steeply declining, stone staircase. They seemed to be in some sort of narrow chasm or gorge and in the moonlight they could see rocky outcrops below them, above them and on the other side of the gorge, about fifty yards away. Moss and lichen grew down the face of the rock and long, thick branches of ivy hung like tendrils on all sides. If Polly looked towards where the river should be, she saw nothing, so narrow and concealed was the gorge. They could not see what was below, but slowly, and with some care, as the rock was slippery, they made their way down the stone steps. The steps ended on a granite ledge, suspended high in the air, and they saw, with some fear, that the only way to scale the vertical cliff was by a wooden ladder, its rungs protruding over the ledge.

"Hope he mended this ladder," whispered Efrem, "but still, I suppose it means we are on right track. I know there is a ladder to Doryty's harbour. He told us about it."

At the bottom of the ladder it was clear they had found the Doryty; it deposited them on a wooden jetty in a little, extraordinary harbour. They could see stone, single storey buildings with lights burning, and a small boat was moored to a wooden jetty, close by the sheer face of rock rising up the side of the gorge. Her mast was nearly hitting the rock face. She was moving softly, as the breeze made the black water rise and fall, rise and fall. A small bridge could be seen, built across the black water below and leading to another jetty; a narrow jetty which was built out from the stone rock face. Copper rings were fastened to the stone, some glinting as moonlight caught them; thick ropes lay curled like snake charmer's baskets, and an anchor was perched on its side. A brown sail was hung from a post and gently flapping, pulling on the ropes which tethered it. At the far end of the jetty stood some barrels which had been made into flower gardens and even in the dark, Polly could see that flowers were spilling over the sides. There were boxes of all sizes, some piled neatly, some fallen over and their contents of metal tools, nails, tins and ropes strewn in heaps, the metal glinting and reflecting the moonlight. Tins of varnish or paint were stacked under the windows and a basket of wild garlic flowers, like a collection of white snowballs, was lying on a table near the door.

Looking away from the tiny harbour and Doryty, the children saw a small house, partly built into the stone wall, but with a room's width extending forwards. It looked a well-kept house, with more flower pots stood on the window sills and by the door, but it also looked like a working house, as heavy tools were leant against the front wall: a crow bar, a pick and an axe. One end of the brown, flapping sail was hung on a hook at the corner of the cottage.

"It's the middle of the night Efrem, what do we do now?" asked Polly, as they crept across the bridge towards the house. The bridge creaked and groaned under their weight.

"Shhh. Hold still a minute. We could shock them, coming in the middle of the night," he replied and they stopped still on the bridge, uncertain about what to do. The Captain, Efrem knew, was not the friendliest of men and he could not quite envisage the conversation they would have, being woken up at two in the morning. But, curiously, the windows of the ground floor shone with light.

The children had little time to wonder what to do, as a dog started to bark in the house, having heard the unusual footsteps on the bridge. The children stood still, holding the rope hand-rail tightly and hardly daring to breathe.

The door opened and an elderly woman, dressed in a long blue dress with a white apron and a mass of greying, untidy hair, peered into the darkness.

"Hello?" she called questioningly and was about to shut the door, presuming the collie dog had barked at a passing fox or similar, when Efrem summoned up his courage and called back.

"Hello, Lady Dotty."

No miner knew the actual name of the Captain's wife as she was never on the weekly trip, so no one, known to Efrem, had ever met her. The Captain sometimes spoke of Lady Dotty and most presumed he was referring either to his wife or his boat, the Doryty, or both. Efrem hoped this was the Captain's wife and he had not offended her.

"Lady," he called, "It is Efrem Tremellin and my good friend Polly. We are from down the river. We are sorry to disturb you so late at night, but I have been asked to find out why the boat..." and he pointed towards the softly moving boat, "does not come...we are sorry to disturb," he added, his nerves beginning to fail.

The lady walked further out onto the jetty and the collie dog bounded past her, rushing to greet the children, jumping up at them excitedly, his tail banging against the rope hand-rail and shaking the bridge. Behind him the light from the kitchen illuminated the wooden jetty and the copper rings shone, as if someone had strung welcoming fairy lights along the cliff face.

"Tremellin?" she asked, "from Latchley?"

"Aye, that is right. We have had some terrible trouble with the theri and..."

Efrem had no time to finish his explanation as Lady Dotty ran towards him and hugged him tight. "Efrem Tremellin. I have been wondering when someone would come. I have heard of your family. I have been hoping someone would come. I have not known what to do. Please, please come in. Polly, did you say? Oh Polly, dear, please come in. I have needed help so much…" She spoke very quickly and not always clearly, but it was evident that she was upset and that she welcomed her night time visitors. "He's had an accident, two, no three, weeks ago now, trying to clear the trees and whatsoever….he's been so poorly," she pulled on Polly's hand and led her into the cottage, talking all the time. " Oh, I have been hoping someone…Polly, you said…oh come in, my dears, do come in…he might be asleep."

Inside, the Captain, far from being the dominating man Efrem remembered, was sat in an armchair by a roaring wood fire. He had a blanket over him and was dozing, his grey head fallen forwards on his chest, so he looked uncomfortable. His collie dog had run back inside, after loudly greeting the visitors, to sit with his head resting on the knee of his beloved master.

"What's the matter?" Polly whispered.

"He fell, deary. He fell trying to clear the trees and has been like this ever since," Lady Dotty pushed her unruly curls out of her eyes.

"How is he hurt?"

"I do think it's his heart, dear. He sleeps most all the time and is so weak, like a kitten."

"Have you had a doctor? Has he been to hospital?" Polly asked her voice and hands beginning to tremble slightly.

The Captain's wife looked blankly at Polly, not recognising such ideas or words. It seemed clear to Polly he had received no medical attention.

"He's bad, dear, he's bad and he's old. I know," Lady Dotty murmured, pulling the blanket higher around her husband's shoulders, "I just don't know what to do..."

"I could bring my mother," said Efrem, "she would know what to do."

"Could you? Would she come? Aye, please do, if she would be so kind," said Lady Dotty, beaming a toothless smile at Efrem, "he's so strong, but he fell, my dears, he fell...maybe two weeks ago now. He struggled back here. It was the first I knew of it! He came in and just said he wanted to sit down...and he has hardly got up since, oh my dears..." she explained, looking sadly at her sleeping husband, her words exhausted.

The room was warm and colourful, like Efrem's kitchen. Tools and jars of stored fruit covered every shelf and washing hung from the ceiling and over the range. There was the same sweet smell of theri and garlic, slightly masked by the smell of paint or varnish. It was a muddled kitchen and Polly could see it would normally be a happy, thriving place of work and homeliness, but tonight sadness dampened the warmth. "I can bring my mother tomorrow night, Lady Dotty, I will bring her."

"Oh, thank you. Now, you need soup and you sit down here. I know something about the boat."

She brought them the same soup Polly had tasted at Efrem's house in the tree, only this time, Polly did not spoil it by pouring thick treacle over it, even though she was again offered a similar large, blue jug, with the thick, black liquid moving like oil inside. Efrem tipped half a jug into his soup and swirled it around with a spoon, until it became a brown colour, like estuary mud.

"The Cap'n found that the river was blocked," Lady Dotty began, lowering herself exhaustedly into a chair, "well, not so much the main river, but our inlet is blocked, so the boat cannot pass. We have no idea why or who blocked the river. Who would do such a thing?" she cried out, only to look anxiously at her husband, for fear she had waked him. More quietly she continued, "the way is blocked with many trees, he said. I have not seen myself, but he was clearing it, a bit every day…then he fell and…here we are," she gestured towards her husband.

"So, the boat has not been able to pass the fallen trees?" asked Efrem, remembering why they had come. It did not sound like a difficult problem to overcome and his spirits lifted at the prospect of returning with definite news.

"No, not fallen trees, my dear, the Cap'n said they were like a mesh, a built jigsaw of trees and branches, all intertwined, like... plaiting. That's how he described it to me," and she threaded her fingers together to illustrate what she was saying, "like someone had made a big basket out of the trees. I know that sounds silly... It's causing quite a lot of water to back up too...the water in the harbour is rising...was a rare mess, he said."

"Where is this? "asked Efrem.

"Maybe half a mile down from here, towards the main river, dear. The water level here, by the house even, has risen... We are so worried that the house will flood! Who would do such a thing?"

The Captain stirred in his armchair and all three turned to face him. He opened his eyes and smacked his lips as if he was thirsty. He peered at the children as his wife placed a glass of water to his lips. "Who are you?" he asked, belligerently, but so quietly that he was not at all frightening. "Who are you?"

"Efrem Tremellin, Sir, and Polly, we are here to see if we can help with the Doryty," said Efrem, speaking loudly, as if the Captain was deaf.

"I can't move her," he murmured, "and I'm not hard of hearing either. Can you move her? Have you come to help?" The fiery Captain sounded frustrated and so sad, it made Polly want to reassure him.

"We can help you to move her," said Polly, hoping to sound optimistic, "when you are better."

"Mmmm," the Captain replied, "I need to be up and moving them trees," and he tried to stand by pushing his arms down heavily on the arm chair. It was too much effort for him and his arms shook; with a slight moan, he lowered himself back into the chair. “Need to get up,” he growled, as fiercely as he could, to no one in particular.

“Aye, deary, aye. You shall be up soon. It is the middle of the night now…so get some rest and then you can be up and about it,” murmured his wife, re folding the fallen blanket. She looked back and her eyes were full of worry, and pleading.

“So when can...” the Captain began to ask, looking at the children, but his head fell forwards, very softly, and he slept.

Chapter Ten

It was a couple of evenings later that Polly returned to the Tremellin's home. Efrem and Polly had walked home quietly that night. The moon had gone down and they had used the electric torch to negotiate their way over roots and stones. Efrem had forgotten about his fear of it. The visit had been sobering and they were both lost in their own thoughts. The Captain had looked so unwell that they felt worried for him and uneasy about intruding. Also, somehow, the devotion of his dog, sitting so calmly beside him as he slept, was upsetting. It all felt like they had stumbled into a situation too big, too serious and adult for them to be able to help and it took away all sense of adventure they might have had. The Captain had dribbled and there had been a smell of urine about him, which had made them reluctant to go too close to him, although they felt they should have been able to help him more, talk to him more and wished they had not backed away. Of course, Efrem's mother could be taken to help the Captain, that was quite straightforward, but they were unsure about his description of the dam, was he confused? Was it an excuse? They knew that to find out, they would have to follow the tributary, down from Doryty's harbour towards the Tamar. Trees could be moved surely! They did not know if anything could be done to help the Captain...

Polly had arrived during another bout of clattering and Efrem's mother and sisters were in the kitchen, but Efrem and his father were trying to stop the booming and clattering which was rebounding from the walls of the kitchen. No one could talk, they just stood still and waited, looking at the door and walls and hoping the whole place would not cave in. Eventually the sounds like someone was hitting the roof with a battering ram and metal dustbins were being flung with force against tree trunks, began to lessen, Alba turned to Polly, " Marfa has been to see the Cap'n, thank you for that. Efrem showed her the way and although she was so scared..."

"Terrified!" said Mistress Tremellin with a shudder.

"She did go," continued Alba, smiling proudly at her Ma, "but he is not strong, she says and he is fretting about the boat."

"I took some tonic and lots of allium soup and vegetables. I will go back, though it is a trial to walk so far and into such strange woodland. I think it helped Lady Dotty just to have someone to talk to. We washed him and he ate quite a bowlful of soup," she turned to point towards the corner of the kitchen, "she asked if we could look after his dog as he was an added worry to her." Mistress Tremellin turned to her cooking. Now the booming had died away Polly noticed the collie dog, sat in the dark corner, looking subdued and frightened.

"Oh look at him," she cried, "is he scared of the noise?"

"Not just the noise," said Alba, stroking his ears, "he is so upset. He doesn't seem interested in anything...we can't make him eat, even." The dog did look sad, or frightened or unwell: it was hard to say which. His ears were down and his head lolled slightly. He was not the bright athlete with shining eyes who had rushed to greet them at the harbour.

The door at the back of the kitchen opened and a gust of warm, sweet smelling air came into the room. Efrem and his father almost seemed to stumble inside, " Oh, it's not so good, Ma," said Master Tremellin, crossing to his wife and putting one arm around her shoulder, comfortingly, " the Big Un is too full, we just had to let most of it go...just opened the pipes and let it all flood out." He wiped his blackened hands down his breeches. He was breathing hard and his face shone with sweat.

"You had to do what you had to do," said his wife, nodding her head at him to affirm his actions and passing him a towel to rub the treacle and oil from his face, "we need to be safe and so if theri has to go, it has to go. No other way."

Of course, she was partly right and partly wrong, and she knew it. They had to release the pressure of the treacle to avoid an explosion and possible damage to their homes or even their lives, but they also could not continue to survive without being able to sell their produce, their dark, sweet, thick and valuable treacle. They were treacle miners and had little future without being able to sell. They knew that each release of treacle into the soil under the wood, brought nearer the day they would have to leave their home, to seek a living elsewhere.

Polly sat down beside the dog and tried to console him, "what's his name?" she asked.

"Oh Cap'n called him collie dog, just that. Collie dog," said Mistress Tremellin, "so we call him that, I just calls, 'Collie' and he comes, not very quickly. He is missing his master, we think."

"We hope to find this blockage, Polly," said Efrem, "we've been talking about going tomorrow night."

"Yes," nodded Master Tremellin, "the sooner, the better. We are getting a group together."

"Needs to be dark, Pater," Mistress Tremellin said, twisting her curls in her fingers. She looked very nervous about the idea, but having made one journey herself and survived, she could only agree to another expedition to try to free the Doryty. She was cutting the white roots of wild garlic and adding them to a pot which contained green herbs, unrecognisable to Polly, and wielding the knife in a very determined way as she thought.

"Efrem and Alba can go with the group, but the girlies need to stay home with me," she said, more to herself than anyone else.

"Marfa," cried Mabel, "I am strong and can help surely!" with this she picked up a large wooden box and to show her strength, lifted it above her head. The lid opened and a flurry of cloths and tea towels fell like snow all around her, one staying on her head and covering her face entirely.

"See?" she cried from behind a veil of tea towel. The family laughed "You and Carita will be vital here," said their father, "if the clattering should start, I need you to run to Master Penn...will you do that?"

"Certainly, Pa," said Carita, from her seat at the table. Mabel slumped to the floor, "Hrrmph."

Chapter Eleven

The night-time trip to find the barrier in the tributary was not without incident. Two elderly miners turned back once they had entered a part of the forest unknown to them; Alba visibly shook with fear and had to be encouraged by Polly; even the jibes and taunts from Efrem could not make her carry on into the forest and away from all she regarded as safe. Master Tremellin was stern faced as he led the way along the rutted pathway and over the strewn trees in the treacle black forest: he was possibly trying hard to not show his fear, his eyes fixed ahead, the lantern held high. The party of ten eventually descended the cliff face, clambered down the ladder, over the bridge and reverently entered the cottage to speak to Lady Dotty. They were all wide eyed with amazement at the sight of the little harbour and the nodding boat.

"He is no better. He sleeps all the day, but he so wants the Doryty to sail. He is feeling so guilty and sorry for you all. He feels it so deep, my dears," Lady Dotty murmured, clasping each miner by the hand in welcome.

"We can make the Doryty sail again," reassured Master Tremellin, handing over a basket of food prepared by his wife, "let me just shake the Cap'n by the hand and we shall set off to look for this blockage."

Master Tremellin shook the sleeping Captain's hand and the old man woke and looked up at him, with surprised eyes, but eyes which showed, despite his physical frailty, that he was keenly aware and alert.

"You've come to take away those fearsome trees?" he asked, "I am sorry I cannot help today...but maybe I can help tomorrow," the Captain was trying hard to speak in the business like tone of voice he used when in charge of his boat, "it will take you some time to move them all. I do honestly think they were being replaced as quickly as I pulled them free. I have never seen anything like it! Do you have some muscle between you?" he looked around the room at the gathered group of miners.

"Aye, there are ten of us here to see what needs to be done, Cap'n. You rest and we shall see you at the helm of Doryty in no time, Sir," said Master Tremellin, adopting the same formal and respectful tone as if they were negotiating a transaction at the weir.

"Just go towards the Tamar and you shall see the thing. I will help you drag some of those trees away tomorrow. I'll bring my heaviest crow bar."

"Aye, you will, now rest, Sir. We shall keep you informed, do not fret."

The group discovered the barrier about half a mile down the small tributary. First, they came across a pond, where it seemed the stream had broken its banks. They were walking in a soggy soup of water and long grass, newly flooded, and it was hard to see any defined banks to the stream. They made slow progress and it was clear that the terrain had been unnaturally altered to create a new, shallow pond. It was eerily quiet. Some trees had been felled, leaving a sharp point facing skyward. Other trees stood, part felled, like giant egg timers, their yellow sap and wood shining bright against their bark. Black and white photographs of battle fields in history books came into Polly's mind: mud, trees lying at strange angles or severed in half but still standing in pools of water and bleak, sad greyness. The similarity of that devastation with the sight before her was increased by the cold, wet mist reaching inland from the Tamar. She was chilled and scared.

At the foot of the pond there was a dam. It stood about six feet tall and was a complicated fretwork of large trunks, twigs, smaller branches and leaves, all intertwined and threaded. The miners gasped, “who would do this?” murmured Master Tremellin.

Efrem leaned across the dam, his legs knee deep in water, and pulled at a branch…it did not move…it was threaded and crossed by other branches and twigs and was so surely fixed as if it had been nailed into place.

“Whatever this is and whoever done it…it’s solid, Pa,” he said between gasps, “each piece seems to be knitted together!”

All the miners tried to pull pieces of wood from the dam and, after snapping branches and much strenuous pulling, some smaller pieces came free, but a half hour of work saw little change in the strength of the structure.

“We need tools,” stammered another miner, “we need to come back with saws and craws and more men!” The group had retreated to some dry ground and were sat, staring with amazement at the intricate structure. "We'll come tomorrow with more tools," said Efrem's father.

"And thick gloves," said Efrem, looking at his bleeding and blistered hands. They all felt overawed and threatened by the tangled barrier which appeared to have been built on purpose. Why?

"We can't do more tonight," Master Tremellin agreed and carefully, negotiating the flood waters and felled trees, they all made their way home.

Chapter Twelve

Polly could not slip out of the house every night. Although she waited until her parents were fast asleep, she still had to be very careful and not allow a door to bang, or forget to put away suspiciously muddy boots...it also made her very tired.

Maybe it was her tiredness which caused her to burst into tears when her parents told her they had news.

"The mining company, Polly, they have found copper under the wood, enough to make it viable for them to mine," said her mother, very gently, over dinner.

"So...what does that mean?" asked Polly, aware of a scream of panic in her head.

"They have offered us a good price to buy the wood. It's enough for us to be able to stay here. We won't need to move, so it's good news," Lara replied, smiling with her mouth, but not her eyes.

"So, the wood will go...it will become a mine?" Polly's voice rose, "It's that Mr Dominus, isn't it?"

Polly's mother reached across to hold her hand. "Yes, the wood won't be ours, but we can stay here, it's not all bad."

"Why won't he just go away? "

"Mr Dominus is just working for the company, it isn't really his fault, Polly. And we have until the end of April to enjoy the wood...it's ours until then," said Polly's father, his voice dejected and grey.

"What?" whispered Polly, "that soon?"

"There are people from Plymouth University who want to save some of the daffodil bulbs, they are so old, so the mining company have to wait until they have finished flowering."

"Hmph," said Lara, "the mining company held up by flowers. "

"But the mining company win in the end, don't they!" screamed Polly and her face crumpled as angry sobs clattered from her chest, her whole body heaving with emotion and fury, " they win, flowers gone, birds gone, foxes gone, fish gone, allium.."

"Allium?" Polly's mother jumped up to console her daughter, "what are you talking about and what can we do?"

"Well, looks like nothing, Mum," sobbed Polly, "looks like you can do nothing!" She knew her anger was misdirected, but she just wanted to lash out and hurt her parents for not being able to save her wood, "you can't do anything!" she shouted into their shocked faces and ran out the room, slamming the door with theatrical grandiosity behind her.

She ran to see Mrs Perkins who sat her down with a cup of tea and slice of parkin, "Ssh, now Polly, this is not your parents' fault."

"I know, but they aren't doing anything to stop it happening! How can we make Mr Dominus go away? How can we stop this happening?" she asked, her sobs lessening as she noisily slurped her tea.

"I don't know. I just wish I could do more. No one will be happy to lose the wood..."

"If he was paid by the miners would he go? Would he be satisfied?"

"I expect so. He only came to look at opening a copper mine when they stopped paying rent. So..." she poured more tea into Polly's cup, "the Doryty must sail, she must."

"Well, they have found the dam and they were going last night to try to demolish it."

"That's what must happen, Polly... Look, look out of the window." Polly looked and on Mrs Perkin's bird table there were two robins pecking at seed, one tiny blue tit and on the ground a grand, brightly coloured cock pheasant. "Look Polly. Those birds won't want to live here anymore, not near a noisy, dirty mine. We will all lose something, Poll." Outside, as if on cue, the blue tit skittered away and the pheasant ran clumsily across the garden and ducked its resplendent head of green, red and white, under the gate, making a guttural squawk as it fled.

"Ah, I know," said Polly, feeling guilty about her rather selfish reaction to the loss of the wood, "but I just don't know how to help...apart from pulling down the dam."

"Then go," said Mrs Perkins, "go and pull down the dam."

Polly smiled and picking up a second slice of cake with a mischievous grin she walked towards the door, "Yes, that dam is coming down, Mrs P!" And she ran out the room, calling from the garden, "thanks for the cake!"

Later that night, when the mist seemed to form itself into dark silhouettes walking quietly beneath her window, Polly stole out of her house, wrapped in a thick waterproof coat and carrying wellington boots. When the group dared to talk, a little after entering the dark forest, she found them all excited and upbeat.

"We cleared so much last night, Polly, It was hard work...look at my hands!" and Polly shone her torch on his bandaged hands, "but we can clear it. A few more nights and we can set Doryty free," he laughed.

The group had grown since the first night and even though they were carrying heavy tools, axes, saws and crowbars, they were a positive group and the cool, dark night around them was filled with their happy whisperings, like bubbles of colour blown in the air. Polly's despair lifted. They called in to greet the Captain and ask about his health, before making their way through the flooded wasteland to the dam. He was stood at the doorway, leaning on his wife and smiling, " well done, well done," he whispered to each miner as they passed, nodding his head and smiling his gratitude. It took all his energy to stay upright and smiling until the last of the group, a young miner called Jan walked past.

"Good lad," he whispered, putting his hand out to shake the hand of the youth. Jan put down his heavy bag of tools and extended his hand. "I know how to sail, Sir," he said, "should you need help with the boat...when the dam is cleared...I know she's your boat...but if you need help..."

"Kind offer, lad, kind offer, but I will be up and about in the next couple of days. I'm not sure, with respect, if anyone else can sail the Doryty."

"Oh of course," replied Jan, his eyes meeting the Captain's, "but if you need help getting her ready to sail...I can help you, Sir."

"Bear it in mind, lad, bear it in mind," and the Captain nodded his head at Jan, before turning and, leaning more heavily on his wife, made his way back to the comfort of the fire and his chair.

The group picked their way towards the dam, avoiding the deepest flood waters and fallen trees. Master Tremellin was the first to notice that things were not as they had left them. He held his lantern high in the air and the group stopped behind him, "where is the pile of wood we took from the dam?"

"There," said an old miner, "to your right…but…half of it is gone!"

"Someone has spread it all over the place," said Master Tremellin and the group made their way to the pile of wood which had been taken from the dam, with great effort, the previous night. Branches were scattered around haphazardly. "Well, it doesn't matter, let's just get on with taking down the dam," said Efrem.

"But I don't understand who would want to create such a mess. The Captain has certainly not been down here."

"Pa!" cried Efrem, "Pater, look at the dam!" The miners all moved towards the mass of branches and twigs stretching across the tributary. Polly did not understand why they were confused, until the miners began to pull on the interlocked branches.

"It's been rebuilt!" cried Jan, "I took all that part down yesterday night, I know I did!"

"Aye," said another voice from a miner who was climbing to stand on the top of the dam, his arms spread wide for balance, "we took this bit down too...some branches we took out have been replaced."

"What?"

"Who would…?"

The miners were shocked and instantly felt vulnerable in the face of an unknown enemy who was seeking to undo their good work.

"Who would replace it?"

"Who wants to stop Doryty sailing?"

Their voices were hushed as they became aware that whoever was working against them could be in the forest now, could be watching them now.

"What do we do?" whispered Polly, her heart beating quickly and her breath coming in short gasps," what do we do?"

"Pull it down!" shouted an elderly miner, shattering the quiet and startling them all, "pull it down again. Work harder!"

"I suppose that's all we can do?" murmured Master Tremellin and with a cry he slammed a heavy axe down on a thick branch, splitting it in two. A long piece of wood fell loudly into the water and the group shouted and cheered: "Come on! To work!"

With much effort the dam was again partly demolished and the branches, twigs and wet grasses were formed into a pile by the side of the pond. The water level began to drop as the river water flowed unrestrained and with some pride in their work the group agreed to finish the job the next night.

However, the following night again brought disappointment and concern to the hard working miners, as the pile had again been strewn around the side of the pond, with branches dragged back and intertwined once more into the fabric of the dam and others dropped as if someone had been disturbed in the process of carrying the branch back. They were all shocked and felt unnerved and anxious about being threatened by unknown people who seemed to want to take away their livelihood. The treacle miners had never sought conflict and had always preferred to lead their secretive, hidden lives in peace.

"Who is doing this to us?" murmured Jan, "why do they want to block the river?"

"It's causing flooding, as well as stopping Doryty. Why would they want to do it?" asked Efrem, voicing the questions they all wanted answered. "It could flood the Captain's house soon."

Jan began to drag a branch from the dam and Master Tremellin laid a hand on his arm, holding him, "don't bother, lad. Every night the dam is rebuilt. We need to know why and we need to stop them. It's no good just taking it down every night."

"I don't want trouble," said an elderly miner, "I can't understand who these people are, but, Master Tremellin, I don't want any fighting or violence. "

The group all murmured their agreement, nodding their heads. They stood together, in a huddle, very aware that they could be being watched and spoke in whispers.

"What can we do?"

"Just talk to them? Ask what they want."

"You mean show ourselves to people!"

"Aye."

"Aye."

"It's all we can do…tomorrow night."

"Yes, we wait and watch and then talk to them."

The group all nervously agreed and set about finding hiding places so they could return the following night and watch.

"I can't join you," said Polly, who was not at all keen about meeting whoever was blocking the river.

"Probably best you don't come. Nor Alba, nor you Efrem," said Master Tremellin, "No," he repeated, placing his hand on Efrem's shoulder, as he began to complain, "you stay home. Look after the pipes. Someone has to."

The following night there was heavy rain, which suited the nervous miners, as it dulled the sound of their footsteps as they made their way through the village, along the forest track and through the harbour to the flooded pond and dam. They did not tell the Captain about the dam being rebuilt each night. No one wanted to worry him.

They sat or knelt, behind trees, in little depressions in the bank, behind stumps covered with ivy: they were good at hiding. They watched, their eyes fastened on the pile of timber they had removed and the spiky dam itself. They strained their ears to listen, but the heavy rain was splashing on the pond and in the river, covering all sound.

It was Jan who first saw them. He nudged the two men hidden with him, behind the wide pine tree, "what is that?" he whispered. The long grass near the pile of timber was moving and it looked as if someone was crawling through the grass, parting it before them, but not tall enough to be seen.

They held their breath and watched.

From another direction, near the bank of the river and the dam, they saw a dark shadow move towards the pile of wood, so low Jan thought the person was slithering on their belly.

With a slight clatter of falling wood, the being came into full view as it crawled up the wood pile and opening its mouth wide, began to drag a heavy branch from the top.

"What?" shouted Jan, jumping out from his hiding place.

Another miner appeared from opposite him, "it's an animal!" he shouted, running towards the dark shape. They could not see the creature clearly, but saw enough to realise it was about two feet long, had a strange, rounded tail and a large mouth and jaw line. The animal dropped the branch in alarm and along with the second creature, both ran awkwardly to the side of the pond, their strange tails slapping the muddy ground, and slipped into the grey water and disappeared.

"Animals!" repeated Jan, wading through the flooded grass to peer into the pond, "Hey, everyone!" he yelled, "come out, its animals taking down the dam....I can't believe what I have seen."

The wet group all emerged from their misty hiding places and looked at Jan and the pond, which was now perfectly still; there were no ripples or waves to show that two strange animals were now somewhere below the surface. No one had ever seen such creatures before and for many long moments, no one spoke. They just stared at the water, as the rain soaked their clothes and hair.

It was decided that they should discuss their next move back in their own wood, once everyone had changed their wet clothes and drunk something warm. They met in the Tremellins' kitchen and Efrem told Polly about the conversation when they met the next day. Efrem was searching for early primroses and Alba was carrying wood back to the house for the fire.

"Polly, there are two fearsome animals building that dam. Jan actually saw one of them...this close to him," and he held his hands a few inches apart, "no one knows what they are, but they have mouths and jaws big enough to hold a whole tree trunk!" and again Efrem showed the size, this time, by spreading his arms as wide as possible.

"What?" said Polly, not believing him at all, "Animals? They saw them?"

"Yes, huge, fierce animals...they drag the wood in their mouths."

"Drag the wood?" Polly's mind swirled...there were animals which built dams and dragged wood: beavers. But did beavers live in this country? Near here? She did not mention her thoughts to Efrem.

"So what are they going to do?" she asked.

"Well," said Efrem, his eyes shining with excitement, "we are all going tonight...come, if you can...and we are going to set traps."

"Traps...what to kill them?"

"Oh no, we are going to just catch them."

"How...you said they were strong...and fierce."

Efrem bent down to pick a bunch of primroses and throw them in his basket, "we are going to take shovels and dig some big holes, pits...and then we are going to fill them with theri!"

Polly laughed, "theri, why on earth..." but she stopped quickly when she saw Efrem's rather hurt and serious expression.

"The animals will get caught in the theri. It won't hurt them, but they will be caught," he explained a little reluctantly. "It's very sticky... and we will dig deep holes..."

"But then what will you do with them?"

"Oh, I don't know. We haven't solved everything yet. At least they can be stopped from building the dam...do you have a better idea?"

"Oh no, Efrem. No. It's a great idea and I will come with you."

Chapter Thirteen

Polly discussed the dam with her friend, Will, in school.

"Ever heard of the river being dammed, Will?" she asked, as they sat in the refectory, eating macaroni cheese.

"Rivers are dammed for all sorts of reasons I expect, there are weirs everywhere, aren't there? Reservoirs?"

"No, the Tamar. Have you heard of it being dammed?"

"Like I said, Poll, there are ancient weirs everywhere. We swim beside one...near you...that tumbledown place, you know."

"But they were all built in the time of the copper and tin mines, weren't they. They are built of stone and just ruins now. Have you heard of it being dammed recently?" she pursued her questioning, trying to sound nonchalant and uncaring about the answer.

"You got Maths next?" Will called to a boy sat behind them, obviously bored with the conversation.

"Yeah," he replied, "want to come with me, I need to go to my locker first." Will forced two huge mouthfuls of pasta into his mouth and, still eating, began to gather his things and stand up.

"Have you?" asked Polly to his back. Will had grown more confident in school recently and although she should have been pleased that he now did not rely on her so much, at times she felt he was brushing her aside, as if she was the needy unfortunate from a previous life. She was the one who did not quite fit in and was an embarrassment to be with.

"What?"

"Ever heard of someone damming the river, recently. Will. I am just wondering..."

"Only beavers," Will replied, laughing and giving her a look over his shoulder which was meant to convey her insanity. He pushed his way through some over turned chairs and tossed his cutlery into a bucket of bubbly water, placing his plate on a tall pile of dirty crockery streaked with tomato sauce and gravy, which looked in danger of toppling to the floor.

"See ya," he called.

With some frustration, Polly followed him along the crowded corridor towards Maths, even though she had to go to Science, the opposite direction.

"What do you mean beavers?" she asked, pulling at his ruck sac to stop him.

"What?"

"The dam. What do you mean beavers?"

"What are you so worried about? You asked what had dammed the Tamar recently and all I could think of was beavers. My Dad was talking about them...Joe, did you do your homework? Escaped, I think...or were they let loose by animal rights people...not sure," Will replied, turning into his classroom. "See you on the bus, Poll."

At the end of her Science lesson Polly had tentatively asked her teacher about beavers and the Tamar, and was ready to make some excuse for her silly question, but was quite amazed to learn that two beavers had been let loose recently, or escaped...he did not know which, either, and had apparently caused some damage to trees by the Tamar.

At home she researched beavers on the internet and saw pictures of immense, complicated and intricate dams built on rivers and streams. She saw the possible damage caused, especially with regard to the flooding upstream of the dam or "lodge", but also read of the benefit to the environment of such "management of water ways." All the information was from sources in Canada however and she was not at all sure that this could have anything to do with Doryty and her Captain. But, Lady Dotty had been worried about the water level rising and the miners had described the dam as being a complicated framework, like a basket...it sounded possible that the animals were the escaped beavers. She knew she could report the dam and its industrious inhabitants to the police or some sort of authority, but what then? Might they find the Doryty? It was unlikely as the harbour was not in sight, but she could not be sure. Her mind, a blurry turmoil of indecision, cleared as she read more and more. She must explain about the animals to Efrem and his family and they must trap and release the beavers. Thus, watching her reading and sitting at the computer, engrossed in what they presumed to be her school work, her parents were relieved that the probable loss of the wood was not affecting Polly as much as they had feared.

Polly succeeded in explaining about the beavers to the Tremellins with a book from the school library and pictures printed from the internet.

"What creatures...look at the tails!" said Master Temellin.

"They look frightening," said Alba, pointing to a picture which showed the beavers' long, tusk like teeth, "I'm not sure I want to see one."

"They'll only keep rebuilding their home, unless we can move them," explained Polly, "there are two of them and they were released from a sanctuary."

"A...what?" questioned Master Tremellin.

"They should not be there, but I don't think they mean you any harm. It's just their home."

"I am astounded," gasped Mistress Tremellin, holding the book closer to her eyes, "who would have thought? Animals as strong as that!"

"And clever, Ma...you should see the dam! It's enormous...so strong!"

The mining community proceeded to dig two deep pits and fill them with sticky theri. They could think of nothing better to do. After two nights, Polly, Efrem and a group of about ten other miners went along the forest track to check the traps. It was clear to them that something was happening, as they could hear a sound, like a child crying or shouting, well before they reached the harbour. Lady Dotty was stood on the jetty, in the dusky light, twisting her hands in her apron, "What is that sound? Is someone hurt?" she asked, grabbing hold of Jan's arm, "the Cap'n is asleep...he hasn't heard it, but oh my dear, it's been crying like that for hours!"

"Stay here," said Jan, a little unnerved himself by the melancholy crying, "we'll go and see...just stay with the Cap'n."

"But you will come back and tell me, dear, you will...only, you see, it has been crying for hours! Hours!"

"Of course," said Jan, twisting his nervous face into a smile.

The group walked more quickly towards the traps and it was soon easy to see that two animals, had fallen into one of the pits. The strange, human like sound was coming from them, as they scrabbled at the sides of the pit, their bristly coats shining with the sticky theri. It was not at all easy releasing the large, scared animals, but with two wooden oars brought down from the harbour, and a large wooden box, they managed to scoop the disorientated creatures into the box before they could co-ordinate their sticky limbs to run away. They were carried, with much straining and sweat, to a shed beside the Captain's house.

"'Tis not their fault," said an elderly miner, peering at them through a crack in the door, "they do need to be washed and fed. "

Lady Dotty was summoned from the house and asked if she had a large bath or trough. With her eyes wide in amazement, as she caught sight of the animals, now licking themselves clean, like over size cats, she pointed behind her to another lean-to outhouse, "there's an old tin bath in there…and…oh my dears…I have lots of wood shavings, mountains of them...if you want to make a bed? The poor things…but I'm not going near them. Do they bite?"

"We are not sure, Lady Dotty, but their teeth are huge. I'll get the bath," said Jan, who was eagerly taking the lead. He filled the bath with water from buckets lowered into the harbour and together with another young miner; they quickly pushed it into the shed, shutting the door quickly behind them. Others tipped wood shavings through a tiny, broken window, to form a soft bed for the creatures and Lady Dotty searched her kitchen for anything they might like to eat: vegetables, stale bread, two trout and a few apples. The beavers made their ungainly way into the tin tub, climbing up the wood shavings and sploshing loudly into the water. Their attempts to swim in the clean water removed most of the black treacle, but, sneaking quickly in and out of the shed, Jan changed the water four times before it began to stay clear, with no trace of theri.

"Let's leave them quiet now," he said and all nodded agreement.

"So," said Efrem, bringing his mind back to the purpose of the capture of the animals, "we can now take down the dam and Doryty can sail?" he asked the question very quietly, as if he was expecting there to be another barrier or obstacle to overcome.

"We can," said Jan and Polly felt a thrill of excitement deep in her stomach. The Doryty could sail! Excitement and relief spread through all the group and the air sparkled with their relief.

"How late is it," asked another miner, "can we start work tonight?" He looked towards the sky where the dawn was just showing as one golden line above the horizon, not enough to brighten the water of the harbour, but enough to indicate that they needed to return home.

"I'll stay here," said Jan. "I can help look after the beavers and get the Doryty ship shape and ready to sail...if that is OK?" He looked towards Lady Dotty, who beamed and clapped her hands together.

"We'll bring tools tomorrow night and take down the dam. Well done everyone...well done!" said another miner and clapping themselves on the back they made their way home, each hugging Lady Dotty as they passed her. "Oh my word," she fluttered, rearranging her apron and hair, "oh my dears, he'll be so pleased. Oh my dears, yes. Yes...tomorrow. Good Night. Be careful. Good Night."

And so, it was only Jan and Lady Dotty who witnessed the final tiny miracle of that wondrous night. Jan worked on the boat for a few more hours, long after Lady Dotty had retired to her bed, until the dawn broke properly on the harbour and the water glistened gold around him. His eyes grew heavy with tiredness and he was heading towards the little house when again he heard the strange crying sound; it was not coming from the shed in which the beavers were sleeping, but from the direction of the dam. Immediately the crying started, it was echoed with louder; more mature crying from the shed and a rhythm of calling or conversation was established. It continued to grow in pace and volume and desperation until it woke Lady Dotty.

"There is another, Jan?" she asked. The crying was immensely sad and becoming almost continuous.

"I think so, stay there," Jan called running towards the dam.

Jan found the baby beaver swimming in the pond above the dam with urgent, splashing movements, as it called and called. He caught it quite easily and wrapped tightly in a towel, to avoid its teeth and sharp nails, took the little one back to the harbour where he briefly showed Lady Dotty, before he pushed it gently into the shed to join its parents.

"Lovely," Lady Dotty sighed, as much from the sight of the little kitten as her pleasure in the quiet which had fallen on the harbour. "There's not another, Jan?" she asked.

"I don't think so. It would be crying too. I am glad it didn't fall into the trap though. That would have scared the little thing to death!"

Leaving the beaver family to sleep and recover from their ordeal, Lady Dotty and Jan returned to the house, talking in whispers, lest they wake the strange, bristly, toothy family snuggled in the wood shavings.

Chapter Fourteen

Spring was established in the wood. The wild garlic was in full flower, like white candy floss on stalks of green. The mossy banks were covered in fluffy cushions of primroses which erupted around the base of the trees and tiny, deep purple violets did their best to squeeze into view and catch the warming sun's rays. Until the dam could be demolished, and the Doryty sail, the treacle continued to flow. Mistress Tremellin had boxes of clothes packed and ready, should the family need to move. Nothing was yet certain as the pipes continued to clatter, bang and thud and the fear caused by the thunderous noise, only increased. Every day more and more precious theri was released into the darkening soil under the wood. The huge cog wheel was turned for one minute, two minutes, five minutes...increasing every day to allow more of the sweet stream to flow away and be lost.

In the house at the edge of the wood change was also being expected and not welcomed. Tempers were frayed and emotions were hard to pin down or explain. Sometimes, the sale of the wood felt a relief to Polly's parents, sometimes it felt like bereavement and sometimes it was a source of irritation and frustration.

"They need to re-do the survey of the land," moaned Polly's father, reading a letter as he stood in the hallway, "they can't arrange this until next week, so another week is lost."

"We can't stay here unless the wood is sold. It sounds like there are doubts now."

"Well, there's no need to be so pessimistic about everything."

"I'm not…I'm being realistic."

"You make it sound like it's my fault."

"I never said anything about it being..."

"Well, I know you don't want to sell the wood to the mining company, neither do I, But we have to."

"I know, why are you saying this?"

Such was the bickering which accompanied the black days of trying hard to achieve something, neither wanted to achieve. At such times Polly quietly left the house, often walking towards the wood. The bickering made her sad, made her feel heavy and tired. She had little control over the situation at home, but she could try to make Mr Dominus go away, by releasing the Doryty and allowing the theri to be sold.

"Efrem!" she called as she saw him, clambering down the bank of the stream with firewood," I can help tonight with the dam. Will you call for me?"

Efrem smiled at his friend. She was an oddity to him, with her strange lanterns and cans of drink which fizzed like the theri in the deepest mine. She knew nothing about the ways of survival so fundamental to him: foraging for food, mining for treacle, hiding in mist and sunlight, but she had been kind to them all and he smiled. "Of course. About thirty will go up there tonight, some to demolish the dam and some to help Jan get the Doryty ready. Others need to stay here in case the pipes start clattering and we also need to get barrels to the weir! When it's time." He smiled again, a warm, open smile, full of relief. "When it's time, the barrels will roll again."

"The barrels will roll," murmured Polly, it sounded magical.

"We can't keep the beavers shut up for ever," said Polly.

"No, we can't. We plan to put them on the boat, when she sails, and let them loose downstream. I'll call for you."

At the harbour Lady Dotty continued to care for her husband. On some good days, he woke early and with bright eyes would ask how the work was progressing to free the boat.

"I'll wander down meself today, lass," he would say, clearly and with determination. However, standing was hard and painful and as his wife pulled on his hands, to help him stand, he groaned and some of the determination and star shine would disappear from his eyes.

"Maybe a bit more of a rest here, lass, another five minutes, and then I'll be up." He would sink back into his comfortable chair, with freshly washed blankets heaped in soft warmth around him, call Collie ...who failed to come...and sleep. Lady Dotty's heart would pound and her eyes fill with tears and she would turn and find fresh work to do, cleaning, laundering and polishing the decks of the stranded Doryty with Jan: work helped her cope with the grief of seeing him so very helpless. Just as the Doryty was so close to sailing, the Captain seemed to be declining.

That afternoon, Polly took two dog crates to the Tremellin's house, to help with the loading of the beavers. As she puffed and panted from exertion, leaning one crate against the kitchen wall and showing Mistress Tremellin how to erect them, she became keenly aware of another victim of the situation. She was disturbed to see Collie dog, who had still not settled at all to life below ground with strangers, creep into the crate. It was as if he wanted to hide away, to make himself as small as possible and escape from his new home. He faced the stone wall.

"He's not happy, is he?" asked Polly, as she went to try to coax him out.

"Oh, we do try to love 'im," said Mabel, squeezing into the crate beside him and wrapping a small blanket over the dog, "He just don't love us..."

A thought came to Polly. "He does prefer to be outside, doesn't he?"

"Oh aye," said Efrem's mother, who was bottling as much dark treacle as she could into huge bottles with corks in the top, "but we can't just let him run free. He would run back to the Cap'n, I think...and she can't manage him, not at the moment. We take him in the wood early morning and late evening, but he's not used to being underground, I do think...and then the clattering....oh my...he shakes and shakes."

"Why don't I have him, look after him, for a while, like?" blurted Polly, not quite clear how she would explain him to her parents. "He could be in the garden; I could walk him more openly. He might be happier."

"We do try to love 'im," Mabel repeated, sticking out her bottom lip.

"Oh I know," said Polly, hugging the little girl until she squealed, "he just needs the air and sunshine. What do you think Ma?" Polly had become used to calling Mistress Tremellin Ma, it felt far friendlier and as everyone called her Ma, regardless of their relationship with her, she had begun to join in.

"Well," murmured Mistress Tremellin, "if you think you can manage him. It is frightful to see him so scared."

So, Polly returned home that evening with a small, slightly cowering collie dog and a long, convoluted story about a friend whose parents were called away suddenly and who had not been able to phone, as they would have done, to ask permission of Polly's parents, and who needed someone to care for their dog for a while, and who were very nice people, and no, they could not be phoned now, as they were in hospital, and yes, she would walk the dog and no, it was not ideal timing as they had so much to organise at the moment.

Her parents' exasperation did disappear when faced with the scared face of Collie and a bed was made for him by the Aga. He began to realise it was quiet in his new home and that the sun shone all day: on his walks and through the window onto his bed. There was no clattering and he could see the sky. Collie dog began to be happy, his ears began to perk up, his eyes shone more brightly and his run was again full of joy and mischief. This all helped to lift the spirits in Polly's home. Collie dog brought a distraction and, although she had not intended this outcome, they all came to rely on the now joyful and bouncy dog to take their minds away from their impending loss. Polly managed to side step questions about how long Collie needed to be with them and the more love Collie showed to the family, the more he received. He had found a home which needed him and he was happy.

Chapter Fifteen

The miners now passed Lady Dotty at least once a night and she became used to seeing them descending the ladder with tools, metal and baskets of food. They had placed lanterns all down the cliff face and hanging from the ladder to guide their nightly excursions and the harbour looked increasingly unreal, like a glittery scene on a Christmas card. The lanterns swayed and their golden light reflected on the water and shining copper. She always rushed out to meet them on the quay, as they crossed the bridge, keen to talk to people and take her mind away from her ailing husband in the room behind her. She chatted, made them all strong cups of peppermint tea or bowls of soup and their visits helped her cope. She not only had her husband to concern her and chill her heart, but the water level was continuing to rise every day. It was only about six inches below the top of the jetty and, from her chair in the kitchen; she could hear it splashing dangerously close. When she dozed off, she was sometimes woken by a dream in which the water lapped around her feet. She would wake with a cold fear, only to find her feet dry in her slippers, with the sound of water swishing and sploshing only a few yards away. If the water breached the sides of the harbour there was nothing to stop it flooding into the house and she knew that they would have to leave, somehow, if this should happen. Young Jan tried to reassure her that the water level could only now drop, as the beavers were safely installed in the shed and the dam was being lowered, but still she worried.

Jan worked hard on the sailing boat: he oiled the workings, hoisted the sail and re wound ropes. Lady Dotty was thrilled to have a young lad to cater for and his work was constantly interrupted with her requests to eat something or stop for a drink. He also spent time sitting beside the Captain, talking to him of the work he was doing, never faltering or appearing awkward when there was no reply. Lady Dotty felt warm inside when she saw him chatting, sat on a stool to the right of the armchair; neither knew if the Captain heard his tales of a rope needing replacing or a screw which was "devilish" hard to move, but Jan chattered as if the Captain followed every word.

The miners, young and old, male and female worked every night to clear the dam. Polly and Efrem worked with them. They used axes to cut large branches and ropes to pull them away. It was not easy, as the branches interlocked, like a web and many times the beavers were cursed for their ingenuity and skill. The water of the pond, upstream from the dam, was grey green in the moonlight and slowly they became aware that the level was dropping, to reveal the long grasses, yellowed by the flood water. Lady Dotty noticed this too, back at the harbour. Holding a lantern high above her, she watched with a smile as the level slowly dropped: water was flowing.

As some cleared the dam, working as quickly as they could, others prepared the sailing boat and yet another group, back in the village, began to transport barrels to the weir as Doryty was coming.

Everyone was busy, everyone sweated and everyone smiled.

The night came when the dam was finally cleared and miners waded deep into the water to check for any logs or trunks which were remaining and could damage the boat.

"It's clear!" shouted a young miner, up to his waist in green- grey water. He had volunteered to dive below the surface to check and dived five times in succession, gasping and pushing back his thick head of hair each time...but always smiling and enthusiastic.

"It's clear!" he yelled, "nothing down here now." The group cheered loudly and clapped and were so excited it seemed they were not sure what do to next, apart from run here or there, clapping and shaking each other by the hand, with large, strong handshakes. Eventually regaining some order, they turned back to the harbour and organised who would sail with the boat and who would go ahead to the village to help take the treacle barrels to the weir. The barrels could roll!

"We've done it Poll," said Efrem, walking beside her back to the harbour. It will take a few journeys to clear all them barrels, but if the boat is sailing, we will clear them. The clattering will stop and we won't have to throw more theri away."

"I'm so pleased," said Polly, panting from exertion, as they clambered the dishevelled and slippery banks back to the harbour. Much of the land close to the tributary had been flooded and because the water had gone down quickly in the end, like a thunderous flood, the ground was slimy and slippery.

Within the hour, on the same night, before the moon rose and the river was in black darkness, the Doryty sailed. Jan took command and along with a crew of two, he gathered in the ropes and with a long oar, pushed the boat away from the wooden jetty, where the miners stood in a jubilant crowd. There were two large crates tied to the deck and covered carefully with old curtains; the beavers were to experience sailing on the Doryty as well, until they could be released by Jan, far downstream of the weir. Their freedom was imminent and he had promised Lady Dotty that he would choose a beautiful, quiet spot for the little family, where they could build their new home undisturbed. Lady Dotty had great affection for the little family, although she never dared to go near them. Although responsible for the near collapse of the miners' livelihoods, they were handled carefully, fed with vegetables and given fresh water for their voyage downstream. Their mournful crying had not been heard again, since the trio were reunited.

The harbour was lit by many lanterns and by the relieved, shining smiles of all who stood and watched the Doryty go...Polly, Efrem and Lady Dotty included.

"Take it steady, Jan," called Master Tremellin.

"Don't put the sails up too early," called another.

"Let her run with the tide, Jan," advised a third, "let the main sail billow and she'll make good time!"

"Remember to let the boom out, when you are running before the wind, Jan...you'll have the current behind ye!"

"I know, I know," shouted back Jan, with a smile and not at all irritated by their advice, "do they not call me, Jan, the sailing man?" The group laughed, with tired hysteria, at his poor joke. Their relief and good spirits combining with fatigue brought on a fit of infectious giggling, which bubbled up in both young girl and sturdy miner alike. They grinned, slapped each other on the back and cheered.

"Jan, Jan the sailing man!" they shouted, as the boat made some movement downstream away from them, jerking slightly as it was pushed away from the jetty.

"Oooh, Jan, do you have your soup?" called Lady Dotty, running out of the cottage with a jug covered with a tea towel. This again caused the group to burst out laughing, holding each other around the shoulder, or slapping their knees. Lady Dotty was not at all sure what she had said which was so funny, but she laughed along with them all, holding the unwanted, steaming jug out towards the departing boat.

The miners, Efrem and Polly left quickly, after the boat was safely underway. There were barrels to be moved and celebrations to be held. Lady Dotty remained alone on the brightly lit jetty, watching the boat turn downstream and begin to pick up speed. She could see Jan as a dark silhouette, holding the tiller in one hand and a length of rope in the other. The sails were not yet hoisted, but they would be when the boat met the wide river Tamar and turned south into the strong current, to begin her voyage to the weir to collect her cargo, and on downstream to Plymouth.

And so she sailed, the Doryty, after many months of imprisonment, she sailed away. Lady Dotty smiled with relief and after waving to the excited miners and then the disappearing figure of

Jan, she turned to re-enter her cottage only to see that her husband, her dear, capable, knowledgeable husband, had also sailed away.

"Oh my dear," murmured Lady Dotty, as she looked across to his armchair from the doorway, the brightness and noise of the occasion suddenly stilled, "and the boat has gone. But maybe you know that?" She went over to him and held his hand tightly. She raised his large, strong and gnarled hand to her lips and kissed it fiercely, "oh my dear."

Chapter Sixteen

Within a few weeks the theri was flowing and being harvested as it had been for many centuries. Barrels were rolled every night initially and Jan became skilled at silently sailing the boat up and down the river, hidden in darkness and mist. He became the new Captain of the Doryty and was treated with the same respect which he, himself, showed towards the boat. He knew how important it had been to the former Captain and never took his position for granted.

The clattering stopped and no more treacle had to be wasted by letting it run freely from pipes under the wood. Pipes could be cleaned until they shone, money changed hands and the Tremellin household again had sovereigns in return for their theri and cupboards full of food.

The Captain was honoured at a funeral held deep in the forest, on a moonlit, spring night and

Polly attended with Collie dog at her heels. Lady Dotty was offered a room in the Tremellin's home, but preferred to stay in her cottage and was thrilled when Jan and his new, young wife asked if they could lodge with her, to be near the boat and their work. She made space for them in the cottage, scrubbed floors and made new curtains and happily spent her days fussing over her new lodgers, cooking and cleaning for them and helping, in her way, to ensure the Doryty continued to sail. Jan brought with him a small pup, a jolly and bouncy spaniel who, along with his young owners, brought joy, fun and a great deal of mischief to the harbour. They all remembered the Captain every day and his meticulous standards with regard to the boat. Jan kept his memory alive by always striving to maintain those standards, polishing, oiling and mending sails: he was so grateful to have the position of "Young Cap'n" and felt the former Cap'n and Lady Dotty deserved all his sweat, enthusiasm and care.

The beavers, after a certain amount of disorientation, set about building a new dam, further down the river, on a small stream which flowed through the grounds of a primary school. The pond they created again raised the water level upstream of their dam. When the stream flooded the school on a Sunday afternoon, the children were delighted to hear that the school was closed for the week as flood water had damaged the electrics. When officials discovered the cause of the flood they diverted enough water to allow both the beavers and the school to co-exist. Still, one week's holiday, while the main hall and gym were scrubbed clean of mud and new carpet lain in the classrooms was a welcome treat.

Chapter Seventeen

One week after the Doryty resumed her sailings and the theri again began to flow, Polly woke to hear her mother sobbing in the kitchen. She cautiously edged her way out of bed and dressed, being careful to avoid the many scars and bruises she had from the hard work of demolishing the dam. She was not sure she wanted to see her mother crying or know why. It would be easier to stay in bed. But she opened the kitchen door to see her mother and father sat at the table, a letter open before them. Her mother was sobbing quietly and her father was staring at the letter as if it was something very dirty.

"Mum?" Polly stayed by the door.

"Oh Poll, I'm sorry. It's OK," said her Mum attempting to smile and looking anything but OK. "Just, just bad news."

"What?" asked Polly, her face pale.

"Mr Dominus has written," said her father. Polly's heart leapt. She had been waiting to hear something of Mr Dominus and longed to hear that, now he was receiving his regular rent from the miners, he would leave her wood alone, safe and sound from him and his destructive mining company. She knew that the Tremellins had paid their rent in full, had even paid all the sovereigns they owed.

"Yes?" asked Polly, her heart lifting and a smile forming on her lips.

"Mr Dominus does not want to buy the wood anymore," her father said, bleakly.

"Yes!" shouted Polly and she jumped in the air, punching her hand above her, "that's wonderful!" But her parents shook their heads sadly, and looked at Polly with guilt.

"No, Poll, it's not good," said her mother.

"Yes, it is! He's gone! We did it!" and Polly skipped to the sink to pour herself some water.

"Did what?" murmured her mother, dabbing at her eyes with a tissue.

"No, Poll," her father's voice sounded irritated and frustrated, "No. Polly. If we can't sell the wood, we must move. We can't stay here. You know that…but it will all be fine…we'll find somewhere…"

Polly's elation crashed around her like bright icicles falling to the ground, like golden daffodils being torn up by black, exhaust belching machines. She dropped the glass in the sink and it smashed.

"He is gone?" she whispered.

"Who?" said her mother, jumping up, "Mr Dominus? Well, yes, he has gone, if you want to put it like that. He doesn't want to buy the wood anymore, that's the point."

"And he doesn't even give us a reason, Lara," said her father, angrily picking up the letter, "he has lost interest, just like that," and he clicked his fingers.

Polly's mind exploded. How could she have thought she could make everything right? Mr Dominus had gone. The wood was safe...but they had to leave...leave the wood. She had changed nothing. How could she be so stupid! Mr Dominus was gone, but that meant they would have to sell their home and leave the wood.

In some despair, fuelled by her naive belief that she could change things, she told Mrs Perkins that the house and wood were going to be sold.

"You have done a good thing though, Miss, don't forget that. The theri mine has been there since Roman days and will continue: the Doryty is sailing."

"I know," said Polly, scuffing her shoes on the rug, "but it's no help to us. I am glad for them. I am...but I don't want to leave...I don't. It's Spring," said Polly, trying to explain the emotions she could not understand herself, "the flowers are coming out, the daffodils, the violets...there are green shoots on the willow tree...you know that bright green?"

"I know," said Mrs Perkins, her eyes filling with tears, "I know."

"Yes, I think you do," said Polly.

Polly maintained her friendship with Efrem and she visited their home, under the tree, almost daily. The Tremellin family were different now, hardworking and productive; they had lost their expressions of anxiety and concern. The barrels were filled weekly and Jan brought them back their sovereigns from Plymouth. The rent was paid, the barrels were moving. The walls had ceased to clatter with a thunder threatening to tear the place apart.

Meanwhile, Polly's family continued to face their own thunder which threatened to force them to leave their home. A 'For Sale' sign was on a post at the entrance to the house and leaflets advertising property for sale again arrived in heavy, brown envelopes every day. The wood was adorned in its spring glory, the daffodils opening to the new, warm sun. Mud had become green grass underfoot and primroses sat like posies on every bank reached by the sun's rays. The daffodils spread throughout the wood, a pale cream and yellow covering, like a silken shawl, which swayed in the breeze and shone in the light.

Efrem, Collie dog and Polly often walked amongst the flowers, finding it impossible not to tread them down, and picked armfuls. The scent was sweet and more delicious than the finest perfume.

"This year, Polly, there seems to be more daffodils...we can pick and pick and not see where we have been."

"I know, it's just covered! I have never seen it quite like this."

"I am so sorry you have to leave."

"Mmm," Polly sighed, smiling at Efrem with gratitude, "I don't know what to say, apart from that I don't want to go."

"You can visit us. Bring Collie dog. "

"Thank you. Oh, I definitely will," she replied, knowing such visits were no compensation for living there, that they would be awkward and strained. She was already beginning to feel a visitor to the wood, as her mind grew accustomed to her future elsewhere.

"You must look after the wood, Efrem. Don't let the new people spoil it, will you?"

"Oh, of course," he replied. "What might they do?"

Both children looked at each other. They had not stopped to think that any new occupants might harm the wood; their lives had been too busy. Of course, the new people could cut it down, Polly thought, burn the wood on their fires and dig up the flowers. As such thoughts raced through her mind, she looked at Efrem's worried face and realised that he would be powerless to stop them. Efrem could not confront them. He lived a blurry life beneath the wood amongst stony tunnels, shining pipes and sweetness.

"Oh, Efrem, they won't touch the wood! Why would they? It's so beautiful, so full of everything that is gorgeous...why would they harm it. They won't. Efrem, it's fine," she blundered, trying to reassure him and herself.

Efrem relaxed a little, but Polly could see she had sown a new fear in him. The future could not be relied upon. Their walk brought them to the very centre of the wood, where daffodils flowed like a waterfall over a bank, hidden from the track. They stopped and sniffed the warm, perfumed air.

"Oh, they smell like the most beautiful thing in the world," Efrem said, "I wish they stayed forever."

"Look," said Polly, holding his arm and turning him towards the bank of hidden daffodils, "they are different. Look how big they are!"

The children stared with some shock at the daffodils hidden behind the bank. In the wood there were quite a few varieties of the flowers; some were wild daffodils with pale, almost white petals. These wild daffodils had a sweet, delicate perfume which could only be smelt at certain times: the sun needed to be rising, the air warming and the dew still hanging on the petals. In other areas of the wood large, dark yellow, brassy flowers bloomed which had probably been planted by farmers in more recent years, aiming to make a profit from the commercial blooms. By the stream a flower called Pheasant Eye grew, only flowering late each spring. This flower had white petals and a dark centre, like the eye of a pheasant and, of all the flowers, gave off the most scent. When the Pheasant Eyes bloomed their fragrance intoxicated the whole wood. There were clumps of daffodils which were more orange, or had petals which were curled, or straight; there were large, thick stemmed flowers which left your hand full of sap when you picked them, and tiny, golden flowers which stood not much higher than the primroses.

But here, on the bank where the children stood, was a covering, a carpet, a multitude of large, different flowers. Each stem supported an unusually big bloom with three circles of petals. The outside ring were big, pale yellow petals, the colour of clotted cream, then there was another circle of petals and these were orange. The orange was not bold or loud, but soft and warm: a warm fire rather than a Christmas clementine. Inside again, at the centre of the bloom was a ring of red, deep crimson: red tiny petals which stood strong and firm, like a fiery crown at the heart of the flower. Each bloom was about five inches wide and they all seemed to be open, looking at the sky and at the children. The scent did not waft up towards the children; it was like a barrier, a scented barrier of sweetness which they crossed as they walked closer. It was like walking from a cold room, shaded from the sun, out into the garden where the warm air was a soothing, scented bath.

"I've never seen these before," said Polly, breathing deeply as she smelled the fragrant, delicious air.

"Nor me," said Efrem, bending to look closely at the open, creamy flower with its crown of fire.

"Maybe, I've not been here before..."

"Maybe," said Efrem, "although I think I have been everywhere in this wood." Efrem looked about him to get his bearings, "Aye, there is the old apple tree and there is the track leading to where we find hazel nuts...I know this bank. I have walked here many a time, but never...."

"No, never...nor me. Never seen...."

Polly and Efrem both felt the world grow a little blurry, a little uncertain. They knew this place, but it had never looked like this before. The air around them was filled with a certain magic, sweet, sweet smells and the sun, as it reflected from the blooms, grew more and more golden.

"It's wonderful," said Polly, stunned into quietness.

"Aye," said Efrem. "It's a place of ...wonder."

Polly, of course, told her parents about the new daffodils in the wood and they told some friends who worked in a nursery nearby and they told some biologists at the local University in Plymouth. Within a few days, many people had visited the wood, always treading carefully as they looked, smelt, examined and discussed the blooms.

Scientists came with sealed bags to collect samples, horticulturists came with trowels and carefully dug up the large bulbs, always asking with great respect if they could "possibly, possibly" have a bulb to examine. People often came back into the house and Polly could hear them discussing the bloom.

"Is it....." one asked, as they compared a photograph of the flower with drawings in old books.

"No, there's no red, see? This one has red. "

"Is it....."

"Or has a new variety evolved. Maybe global warming?"

"No, there are too many. They have been there for years. Must have been, just never flowered..."

"Maybe pollution?"

"Pollution? No. It's the middle of nowhere here! Back of beyond!"

Discussions were animated and not always pleasant to listen to. Polly did not join in, but preferred to find those few quiet moments, when people had gone away with their photographs, drawings, samples and ideas, and sit with Efrem breathing in the deliciousness of the daffodils; trying to clear her mind of the packing cases in the hall, the estate agent leaflets on the table and the dusty, unclean smell of the house as musty wardrobes were emptied and faces were glum.

In between visits from families, looking for a new home, a group of biologists arrived from the

University. There were two men and two women and they all looked excited and purposeful.

"May we have a word?" asked a man who had introduced himself as Professor Brown.

"Of course," said Polly's mother, "I am afraid we are selling the house, so we have been clearing out the cupboards... it's all rather dusty and messy. Do find a chair, if you can. I will make coffee."

"Thank you, thank you," they all mumbled and removed bags and boxes from chairs in order to sit down. The Professor remained standing. After coffee was served and Polly had fetched her father from the barn, where he was trying to make some order of his tools, the Professor spoke with grandeur the words which would change their futures.

"We have identified the daffodil in your wood," he beamed. All the scientists smiled and gasped with excitement. Polly could not feel any great pleasure from the announcement. So what, she thought? She did not like the way other people seemed to have ownership of her daffodils.

"It's an ancient variety which was probably first planted here by the Romans and was thought extinct. It has not been seen anywhere for centuries! Neither here or in Italy."

"Centuries and centuries!" interrupted a young woman, leaning towards Polly's parents, "It was thought lost!" She tapped her clip board with excitement.

"Oh," said Polly's father, nodding his head in appreciation of their efforts and to acknowledge their excitement. "We know it's a beautiful flower. Quite uncanny. It's a beautiful thing to see and to smell. We do wonder why it has flowered now."

Although he did not fully share their enthusiasm for naming the flower, the whole family found it fascinating to think the bulbs had slept, dormant for so long, in the mossy, rich soil of the wood.

"Why have they flowered now? This year?" asked Polly's mother, "It is fascinating. You must have worked hard to trace the flower."

"We don't know why it is flowering now," said the Professor, "and yes, it has taken considerable research to identify this ancient variety. We need to study the circumstances and the weather..."

"and the soil and.." interrupted the young woman.

"Yes, yes," said the Professor, fanning away the interruption with his hand, "you have asked the question we need to answer. Why have they hidden away, dormant, dead in the earth for centuries and now flowered, this year, now...and in such splendour! We don't know the answer, but we want to try to find out."

"It's such an event," continued the Professor, growing more excited, "the bloom was known in Roman times and celebrated for its beauty. Apparently, it was grown near the Emperor's palace and even...although we don't know if this is true, the bulbs were fed over the winter."

"Like we use fertiliser?" asked Polly's father.

"Yes, in a way, from what we have read... but if our translations from Latin are correct they used to feed the bulbs with something sweet, we presume it was like a honey. Their slaves fed and cared for the bulbs and then the flowers. It's fascinating."

"It is," said Polly's mother, "more tea? Coffee?" Their excitement about the flowers only made her feel sadder that they had to leave them to someone else.

"No, we must not hold you up. We know you are busy and thinking of moving and it is actually that we need to talk to you about," said the Professor with an air of seriousness.

Polly's parents exchanged surprised looks.

"We have spoken to the University...we all are employed by the University and we have spoken to the Royal Horticultural Society. We have a proposal for you."

"What, sorry?" murmured Polly's mother, placing new mugs of coffee before the scientists.

"We are in the happy position of being able to buy this house and the wood and conserve it. We would like to buy this property," the Professor announced grandly, as if he was giving the family a wonderful present.

"I can see you wish to conserve the area, but..." said Polly's father, slightly bemused and wrong footed. "It's very good to know it will all be preserved...do speak to our estate agents. I am sure they can help you. It is all up for sale, you know."

"No, no," said the Professor, "I have not explained myself properly. We wish to buy this house and wood and would very much require that you continue to live here, just as now. We do want to study the daffodils, but not in any intrusive way. We absolutely do not want them disturbed too much. We can't put them in danger. No diggers, no disturbance of the land or the soil...just careful studying and watching. We need someone here who we can trust to conserve them. They are too precious to lose, to be interfered with. We will buy the house and wood and you can pay us back...over time."

"You," stammered Polly's mother, "you will buy the house and land and allow us to live here? Am I right? But we can't pay you back...we can't pay the mortgage now!"

"Yes, you can," said the Professor, expansively, throwing his arms wide, "the daffodils are very rare. With careful management they will make you a fortune and you can pay us back. People will pay a fortune, for just one bulb!"

"Just one bulb," interrupted another scientist.

We would like to buy it to ensure you stay," continued the Professor, "We need the wood left alone."

"Left alone," murmured Polly, thinking of the mining and theri, "that sounds very good."

Polly's mother and father were looking at each other and both were beginning to cautiously smile.

"You will buy the property and we will pay you back...a loan?"

"Yes," replied the Professor, pulling out papers from his case, "I have been busy the last couple of days. I have all the paperwork and please do have it all checked with your solicitors. It does mean you won't have to move and I presumed that would be welcome? The daffodils are worth a considerable amount. That's how you can earn money, but it is also why we need the bulbs protected...for science. They need careful management. Most bulbs need to be left season after season..."

Polly, her mother and father were searching each other's eyes. They all smiled in unison and turned to the Professor. "Yes please, we accept!" beamed Polly, "but what is the name of my daffodil? Did it have a name?" Her face was lit with gold.

The Professor smiled, "Well, in Latin, it was called Dulcis Aura. We have seen references to it on old transcripts. We can roughly translate that from the Latin to mean Sweet Breeze or Sweet Air."

"Because of its scent?" exclaimed Polly, quite delighted with the name, "It makes all the air smell sweet!"

"Yes, we presume so. The scent is extraordinary. Sweet air, sweet breeze, sweet something like that. You can understand why they called it Dulcis Aura."

"Dulcis Aura," said Polly, and below her and around her the wood seemed to exhale and breathe, like someone shaking their shoulders, releasing pent up tensions and lifting their face, eventually, to the sun.

Epilogue

A few days later, when the paperwork had been signed and finalised, Polly, her parents and Collie Dog walked up to gaze at the wondrous display of colour which was the Dulcis Aura falling over the bank like creamy, fiery confetti. The warming spring air, which still held some of the chill of the night, was filled with their exquisite scent; white cotton wool mist lifted from the stream and the fields as the air warmed.

Polly stood between her parents, her arms around them both.

"It's such an amazing scent. I can't find words to describe it," said her mother breathing in the deliciousness, "I could stand here all day..."

"It's like the sweetest perfume," said her father, "we owe everything to this flower and the fact it chose to flower now...now, of all times. It's inexplicable. They still don't know why the flowers chose this year to bloom. Amazing…such luck… and the smell…I think it smells like, like burnt sugar."

"Yes, but not quite…It's like something very sweet. It reminds me of pancakes and syrup," laughed her mother.

"I don't know…it's hard to pinpoint," said her father, sniffing the air loudly, like a dog following a scent. They laughed. "Is it sweets or is it butter melting in a pan?"

Polly thought of all that had happened, of pipes underneath their feet and of theri being released to flow into the soil, to soak into the ground below the roots and bulbs of the ancient daffodils...she thought of theri sweetening the soil and of the thin, white daffodil roots, reawakening, reaching out from the bulbs to drink up the sweetness. She imagined the thin, white roots searching through the soil, pushing apart the grains of earth, small stones, slugs and wood lice, growing stronger and thicker. She thought of how the Romans fed their plants with something sweet and of the treacle from Wheal Kitty and the Big 'Un, being released from the pipes to flow into the soil, waking up the dormant bulbs, bringing them back to life. She thought of the wasted theri being not so wasted after all. She imagined the ancient bulbs lying so long: shrivelled, papery, blackened and lifeless under the soil and moss and leaves of the wood, waiting for the sweetness they craved in order to glow and shine and live again.

"I know what they smell like," she announced with certainty.

"Yes?" said her father.

"They smell like treacle."

The sunlight reflected from the dewy, golden petals of the swaying Dulcis Aura; it bounced off the glistening, green leaves and formed tiny prisms of light; distorting perception and creating a rainbow in each drop of water caught in petals and leaves and lacy spiders' webs. Every head of every daffodil was turned to the morning sun, strong and growing stronger.

Deep under the soil, the copper pipes of Latchley Theriaca Dulcis Fodina, the treacle mine, were gently reverberating to the gloopy, sticky flow of theri; there was an occasional sploshing sound, a drip: plink, plink as the dark liquid flowed from one pipe to another, sometimes a whoosh as a wheel was turned to allow the treacle to splash into a barrel, but the treacle was flowing, smoothly and sweetly, the clattering pipes were calm.

A Brief History of the Cornish Treacle Miners

You may well wonder about these extraordinarily secretive people who live under the woods. Are they human? Well, yes, but they have been hidden away from society for so long that they are as different from you and I as it is possible for human beings to be.

Their story begins more than two thousand years ago, when fierce tribes of warriors, the Dumnonii and the Cornovii, fought for control of the tin and copper mines. One small group, who mined for treacle on the Tamar, found it was safer to keep out of these arguments. So they hid themselves away and sold their precious, sweet, sticky, black treacle to both sides.

When the Romans came to Cornwall, the miners enjoyed the relative peace which they brought. The miners learned to speak Latin, and they became a little more adventurous, venturing into the woods of the Tamar Valley, although they soon retreated to the safety of their mines if there was any trouble. They saw the buildings the Romans constructed and the flowers and plants they grew.

They sold their treacle to Roman merchants who paid in gold but who also took rent for the mines which they said belonged to them. The treacle miners didn't like to argue, because a very sharp sword often offends.

Then, with little warning, the Romans left and a new, more savage, tribe called Saxons arrived. They fought against the Dumnonii and Cornovii. The treacle miners responded by hiding away even more and only leaving their subterranean world when they had absolutely no choice. They still sold their treacle but through an intermediary, and at least one Roman stayed on and collected rent payments in gold. He founded a family who, for generations, existed by collecting rent. The miners became skilled in hiding, using nature to camouflage their every act.

This state of affairs lasted for nearly two thousand years, Vikings came and left, travelling up the Tamar to Danescombe , then Normans took over. The miners heard stories about what was going on in the wider world and they felt much safer staying where they were. People fought a war over roses; there was a Civil War, which didn't sound very civil, and a Great War, which didn't sound all that great. The treacle miners heard of the mass emigration of the Cornish copper miners, the Cousin Jacks, who travelled far away: much further away than they could imagine. Not many returned. They heard rumour of one or two returning to Gunnislake, bringing their new wives with them to a new land. But, mainly, the copper mines stayed silent and asleep.

So the miners hid underground in the woods and they only came out at night, or on misty days, to hunt, dig up roots, fish, or move their precious treacle cargo. And that's where you came in.

About the Author

Sally lives in the beautiful Tamar Valley with Keith, her husband and their two dogs, two horses and a ginger cat called Dylan. They raised their sons Jimmy and Charlie, of whom they are so proud, on the family small holding.

Sally taught English in a local secondary school for thirty years and loved working with young people, especially in her role as Head of Sixth Form. She now tutors, writes, cycles, walks in the woods and cares for the diverse animals who live with the family.

The Tamar Valley is stunning and extraordinary: nature merges with the historic ruins of the former, vibrant copper mining industry. Hence woodlands are full of wild daffodils, wild garlic, rivers, streams and also deep, dangerous mine shafts, mine entrances and the remnants of tram ways now leading nowhere. This became the inspiration for the story.

About Blue Poppy Publishing

Blue Poppy Publishing is a very small independent publisher based in Devon. We publish books by local authors for children and adults. Although not a traditional publisher, we are certainly not a vanity publisher. For full details and to explore more of our titles see our website
www.bluepoppypublishing.co.uk

If you enjoyed *A Clattering Beneath the Woods* we would love to hear from you. We know that Sally would love you to write a review on our website, or you can contact us via
info@bluepoppypublishing.co.uk